"There's nothing I'd like more than to toss your interfering ass in jail, Ms. Cruz."

Excitement sizzled head to toe and Claudia flicked her tongue over her lips, pleased beyond all civilized decency when Vincent's gaze briefly dropped to watch. No matter what words he said, what he wanted wasn't her ass in jail but in his bed.

"Always so serious. All work, no play—"

"You want to play, Ms. Cruz?"

A breeze drifted inside her car, bringing with it the smell of city traffic, hot asphalt . . . and *him*. He didn't wear cologne, but the scent of soap, perspiration, and warm skin was heady enough. She shifted restlessly on the seat.

"Do *you*?" She matched his cool tone. "Because I don't play so nice."

His smile faded, lips settling into a thin, grim line. "Neither do I."

Turn the page for rave reviews of
Michele Albert's hot and sexy suspense novels . . .

Her Last Chance is also available as an eBook

TOUGH ENOUGH

"Albert's hot adventure and mystery series steams up with the release of a new tale featuring super-secret Avalon agents. . . ."

—*Romantic Times*

"*Tough Enough* . . . will captivate readers who enjoy a good romantic thriller."

—Romance Junkies

HIDE IN PLAIN SIGHT

"A dangerous man, a clever woman, and a twisty, high-risk chase that kept me up half the night . . . hot, hot, hot!"

—Julia Spencer-Fleming

"Steamy suspense and lots of action . . . a fast-paced thriller that will please fans of Linda Howard and Catherine Coulter."

—*Booklist*

"Amazing. . . . Good romantic suspense is always a pleasure."

—*Romantic Times*

"A compelling tale of lovers on the run. . . ."

—Paperback Reader

ONE WAY OUT

"The outstanding Michele Albert's new adventure is roaring, and the romance sizzles. Settle in for a great ride."

—*Romantic Times*

"Exciting romantic suspense. . . . Action-packed. . . . Michele Albert provides a fine, exhilarating, way-out tale."

—The Best Reviews

"A fast-paced, suspenseful book that's impossible to put down. This book has a kick-ass heroine and a hot, yummy hero. . . . If you like suspense, mystery, and action mixed in with your romance, this is THE book for you!"

—A Romance Review

"Another winner. . . . *One Way Out* is a brilliantly paced story. . . . The chemistry between Alex and Cassie fairly sizzles off the page. . . . A wonderful, one-sitting read that touches both the heart and the funny bone. . . . Snap this one up—you won't be disappointed!"

—Contemporaryromancewriters.com

"[A] fast-paced adventure . . . a zesty read."

—BookPage

"An enjoyable and suspenseful read. . . ."

—All About Romance

"Lots of romantic sparks and witty dialogue. . . ."

—The Romance Reader

MICHELE ALBERT

HER LAST CHANCE

POCKET BOOKS

New York   London   Toronto   Sydney

Pocket Books
A Division of Simon & Schuster, Inc.
1230 Avenue of the Americas
New York, NY 10020

This book is a work of fiction. Names, characters, places, and incidents either are products of the author's imagination or are used fictitiously. Any resemblance to actual events or locales or persons, living or dead, is entirely coincidental.

First Pocket Books paperback edition March 2010

POCKET and colophon are registered trademarks of Simon & Schuster, Inc.

For information about special discounts for bulk purchases, please contact Simon & Schuster Special Sales at 1-866-506-1949 or business@simonandschuster.com.

The Simon & Schuster Speakers Bureau can bring authors to your live event. For more information or to book an event contact the Simon & Schuster Speakers Bureau at 1-866-248-3049 or visit our website at www.simonspeakers.com.

Cover illustration by Craig White

Manufactured in the United States of America

10 9 8 7 6 5 4 3 2 1

ISBN 978-1-4165-3140-1
ISBN 978-1-4391-6800-4 (ebook)

Acknowledgments

For the patience and understanding shown to me over the ups and downs of the last couple years, I would like to sincerely thank my family—especially my husband, Bob, and my son Jerott—as well as my editor, Micki Nuding, and my agent, Pam Ahearn.

If your enemy is secure at all points, be prepared for him. If he is in superior strength, evade him. If your opponent is temperamental, seek to irritate him. Pretend to be weak, that he may grow arrogant. If he is taking his ease, give him no rest. If his forces are united, separate them. If sovereign and subject are in accord, put division between them. Attack him where he is unprepared, appear where you are not expected.

The Art of War, Sun Tzu, fourth century BCE

Chapter One

Monday afternoon, Philadelphia

The sharp click of high heels on Champion and Stone's plank flooring was his first warning that she'd arrived, but Vincent DeLuca knew it was her before he turned to look, before she spoke, before her heavy floral perfume invaded every pore of his skin. He knew because a rush of hot lust swept over him at the exact same moment hairs prickled along his arms and the flesh between his shoulder blades crawled.

Only one woman had ever had such an effect on him.

Vincent stepped back into the main room to face her, since ignoring Claudia Cruz wasn't an option. Everything about her dominated and demanded, and her sinuous strut kicked him into a sensory overload of breasts and hips straining the seams of a red suit, brassy curls, cinnamon-red lipstick so glossy it looked as if she'd just licked her lips, and cold black eyes that met his almost on the level.

"Special Agent DeLuca." Even her voice, low and a little raspy, sent mixed signals of sweet and rough. "I knew I'd find you here."

Here being the wrap-up of his investigation at an art gallery in Philadelphia's tourist-heavy Old City. He'd unlocked the door a few moments ago to admit a FedEx driver, and she must've been outside, watching and waiting for an opportunity to slither inside.

At this point, however, she couldn't cause any trouble. Or at least no more than usual.

"Not surprising, Ms. Cruz," Vincent said. "I'm usually at work when I'm working."

"And hard at work, I'm sure," she murmured, smiling, then trailed a manicured red fingernail down his tie.

The unexpected touch startled him so much that he didn't even think to push her hand away. The rest of him responded quickly, though; his belly tensed before her finger had reached halfway to his belt buckle.

Just as he narrowed his eyes, she stepped out of reach, a humorless smile still curving her lips. "Has anyone ever told you that you're a walking, talking cliché, Mr. FBI Man? Tall, dark, and ever so grim; the black suit and tie; that steely-jawed look, and the stick-up-the-ass posture—it's all—"

"What are you doing here?" His sharp tone made the detective filling out forms by the cash register glance up.

"As if you have to ask." Her gaze moved past Vincent's shoulder to the nearest gallery annex, and she frowned slightly. "Hmmm, is that the manager? It looks like she's been crying. I hope she's not having hysterics, because I'm not too handy with hysterical women."

"That would require compassion, and compassion isn't high on your boss's list of job skills when he hires people like you."

Claudia sent him another slow, maddening smile. "Oh, now, Vincent. You make it sound so . . . ugly."

Her hair was longer than when he'd first met her four months ago, with the loose corkscrew curls styled in an artful disarray, as if she'd just been fucked on an office conference table.

Vincent squelched that thought—and its accompanying visuals—and moved between Claudia and the others, blocking both the curious detective and the gallery manager. Lowering his voice, he said, "Ugly about covers it. And every time you shove your way in where you don't belong, I get more determined to take you down."

"Take me down where?" She feigned innocence. "I'm not that kind of girl, you know."

"Yank my chain one time too many, Ms. Cruz, and you'll find out. This is the third time I've warned you and your kind to keep clear of my investigations, and it's the last."

Something sparked in those dark, assessing eyes, and it wasn't fear or shame or anything remotely remorseful. "Big talk, no action. Ain't that just like a Fed?"

For a moment longer, she held his gaze. When he raised a brow and shrugged, she turned her back and headed toward the manager. The detective—a competent, fiftyish man named Matherson who had pale eyes and thinning brown hair—followed the swing of hips in that tight skirt. Vincent couldn't blame the guy; he'd never managed to look away, either.

After joining Vincent, Matherson leaned over and whispered, "Who the hell is *that*?"

Vincent didn't reply, since any answer would require a long explanation. The investigation was over for now, and as fun as it would be to sic Matherson on Claudia Cruz and watch the fur fly, it still wouldn't be half as entertaining as watching the woman in action.

"Did you hear what I— Vince? You feeling all right?"

Vincent took a deep breath, then ran a hand through his hair, wiping away the perspiration along his upper lip with his sleeve as he did so. "Yeah, I'm good. Just a fever I can't shake."

"Maybe you should see a doctor about it," Matherson said in all seriousness.

"Maybe," Vincent agreed, holding back a smile.

Against a backdrop of expensive paintings, Arnetta Gallagher stood beside an empty display case off the main entryway, only a fraction calmer than when Vincent had arrived. As Claudia touched her arm Arnetta visibly relaxed, assuming she was in the presence of a sympathetic female, an ally.

People were so gullible.

"I had this cousin once who couldn't get rid of a cold." Matherson's voice broke across Vincent's thoughts. "And then one day he dropped dead."

Vincent finally looked away from Claudia. "Thanks for the advice, but this isn't the kind of fever that'll kill me."

Unless a bad case of blue balls suddenly turned fatal. But after four months of dealing with this woman shadowing his thoughts and prowling through his dreams, he doubted the problem could get much worse.

"I hear your day got off to a bad start." Claudia's voice was warm with false concern, and Vincent, brows arched, slipped his hands in his pockets and settled back to watch the show.

Arnetta let out a shaky sigh, then dabbed her mascara-smudged eyes. She was a stately, gray-haired woman who'd worked for Champion and Stone for twenty years, and, as she'd repeatedly told Vincent, nothing like this had ever, ever happened to her before.

"I can't believe this," Arnetta said. "Nothing like this has ever, *ever* happened before. It was there last night, and this morning it was gone and that *toy* left in its place. No alarms, nothing on the cameras—it's as if they slipped in like ghosts!"

Claudia gave Arnetta another comforting pat on

the shoulder of her impeccably tailored tan suit. "I hope it's not too fragile."

"Oh, God, the bronze is so *very* delicate. . . . You can't cart around something that's twenty-five hundred years old like it's part of some Halloween costume. And to make matters worse, it's the only Corinthian helmet we've had in stock for over four years. Ms. Stone is going to be simply furious!"

"It's hardly your fault," Claudia said, soothingly. "I'm sure you've done nothing wrong."

She was fishing for information, but carefully enough that Arnetta would never realize it. Claudia had gambled that talking with Vincent first—even playing up their hostile familiarity—would validate her presence.

The gamble paid off: anger, bewilderment, then worry crossed Arnetta's face before she said, a shade defensively, "I checked over the inventory before I left last night, activated the alarms, and locked up like I always do. I have absolutely *no* idea how they got inside!"

Claudia's gaze darted toward Vincent, then away again when she verified he wasn't making any move to stop her. He had no intention of doing so; he'd had enough experience with this woman, and others like her, to know that he had to pick his battles.

She danced at the very edge of his last nerve, and as much as he wanted to believe he tolerated her intrusions because he was biding his time and waiting for the right moment to strike, it wasn't his only reason.

"Maybe Mr. DeLuca will find something useful on the security data." Claudia paused. "Providing he remembered to take the recordings into evidence."

"Oh, he did. He's a very thorough young man."

"I never doubted it," Claudia said mildly, glancing back at Vincent again and giving a little shrug, as if to say, "Oh, well, I had to ask."

As if he'd let her walk out the door with evidence. Still, her response—and the faint irritation underlying it—almost made him laugh.

Another fifteen minutes passed as Claudia produced more supportive comments designed to prompt Arnetta to spill her guts. Once Claudia had determined that she'd milked the situation for all it was worth—and that Arnetta would be of no real help—she smoothly disengaged and headed back his way, hips swinging, a small smile curving her mouth again.

At her approach, Vincent asked, "Did you get what you wanted, Ms. Cruz?"

"For the most part, Special Agent DeLuca," she answered, matching his mocking, exaggerated politeness. "If I need a little something more, though, I'll be sure to come find you."

As she headed toward the door, Claudia gave Matherson a polite nod, and the detective frowned. Good instincts: the man knew a carnivorous interloper when he saw one, despite a breathtaking distraction of breasts and hips.

Vincent should've just let her walk out the door, but allowing her the last word galled him too much.

"Nice suit there, Ms. Cruz, and I noticed the classy makeup. I thought you people were supposed to downplay your presence."

Matherson opened his mouth to speak, then snapped it shut at Vincent's warning glance.

Claudia turned, and if the dig had offended her, it didn't show. "We people are given a broad range to work with, but the sensitive jobs usually go to the sensible, boring guys like Tiernay."

Vince rubbed the stubble along his jaw. "That would be the sensible, boring guy who blew up a factory and a couple people outside Boston a few months ago, right?"

"I wouldn't know anything about that," Claudia said demurely.

"Of course not." She'd been there, though. Vincent had checked into the situation—as best he could with the Boston cop who'd dodged his more pointed questions.

"It's been great talking with you, Mr. FBI Man, but I gotta go. You have a lot of paperwork to do now, right? Me, I'm off to catch a thief, seeing as how I don't got to deal with all that bureaucratic stuff."

He'd noticed that whenever she was feeling cocky, the *barrio* came out more clearly in her voice—and her comeback jab put them at a stalemate. Again.

"Give it your best shot," Vincent said. "I'll be watching to see if you can deliver, or if you're all flash and no substance."

Suspicion flared, then narrow-eyed annoyance. Then she blew him a kiss and walked out, heels clicking and a little extra swish in those hips.

Heat rolled over him, and he let out his breath, hoping no one noticed he'd been holding it in the first place.

"Who's that young woman?" Arnetta demanded. "Isn't she one of your people?"

Vincent imagined her reaction if he told her the truth: *"That young woman is the human equivalent of a shark. She works for a soulless sonofabitch who thinks he's above the law because he's stinking rich and has powerful friends all around the world. He owns a travel agency that's just a cover for a bunch of mercenaries who also think they can run roughshod over every law in every country. Only these days they call themselves private contractors, not mercenaries."*

Instead, he said, "Nope."

"Oh." She blinked. "Somebody about the insurance, then?"

The woman's distress and confusion radiated off her in waves, pricking his conscience. His day had been lousy, but hers had been much worse, so why was he being such an ass?

"No. She's what you might call a freelancer in art theft recovery."

Arnetta Gallagher wasn't stupid, and every line of her body stiffened with anger. "Then she shouldn't have been here. Why did— You should've stopped her!"

"From doing what, Ms. Gallagher? Listening to you talk? She never once asked you a question. Technically, she's not interfering."

Not enough for him to waste valuable time by causing a situation that would end in another reprimand. He'd discovered the hard way that Cruz might be a handful, but her boss's lawyers posed far more trouble.

"I'm already going to have to explain to Mr. Champion and Ms. Stone that their prized Greek Corinthian helmet has been stolen from under the noses of a senior employee and one of the best security companies in Philadelphia." Anger sharpened Arnetta's soft, refined voice. "I hope you had a very good reason for your actions, and that this woman's presence won't cause me any further trouble."

"It won't." Not for Arnetta; for himself, he couldn't be so sure.

"So why didn't you stop her at the door?" the gallery manager demanded. "You're a federal law enforcement agent. You have the *authority*."

Matherson's frown deepened, but he kept his mouth shut.

"It's nothing you need to worry about. She's on your side. Solving specialized crimes like this often takes a cooperative effort from many investigators, including those in the private sector."

It sounded good, big words and all, and more dignified than explaining the FBI sometimes had to deal with the devil it knew in order to catch the devil it didn't.

Guilt pricked again, and he added gently, "Look, it's been a rough day for you and we're done here. You should have a cup of tea or something before locking up. Try to relax. We'll be in touch if we have any more questions, and we'll keep you posted if anything turns up. That's about all we can do right now."

Arnetta nodded, then reluctantly moved away, still looking a bit lost and frantic. Vincent supposed that if he'd had a chunk of bronze worth nearly two hundred grand disappear on his watch, he'd be a little green around the edges, too.

Once Arnetta was out of earshot, Matherson cleared his throat. "Okay, I'm not sure what just happened here, but that hot little number in red wasn't someone you know?"

"I know her."

The detective shot him a look of exasperation. "But she wasn't authorized personnel."

Matherson had no reason to know about Avalon, Claudia's employer, and he was better off remaining ignorant. People who knew too much occasionally ended up dead. Or simply disappeared. "Somebody's contracted her services. That's all the authorization she needs."

"So she's like a private investigator?"

"You could call it that."

Annoyance flaring, Matherson asked, "So why did you *really* let her walk in here and do whatever the fuck she wanted?"

Vincent shrugged. "Because I've got nothing to work with. She's not one of us, so she doesn't have to operate like us. Maybe she'll get lucky—and when she does, I will."

"Ah-hah." Matherson drew out the word, nodding in understanding. "You're tailing her."

"There's no place her sweet ass goes that I don't hear about it. So that's the plan."

Or half of it; the other half was that he wanted to catch this woman in an illegal act—anything would do, no matter how petty—so he could make an example out of her. That high-handed bastard in Seattle needed to learn an important lesson: no one was above the law, not even the obscenely rich and powerful.

Next to catching this annoying little shit of a thief he'd been chasing up and down the East Coast for months, there was nothing Vincent wanted more than a chance—just one chance—to show Avalon they could no longer ignore the FBI.

Her floral scent still lingered, bringing to mind warm skin and lush female curves, a mouth in wet red lipstick and hair he could grab in both fists.

He blocked the image. Nope, there was nothing more that he wanted. And if he repeated it often enough, he might even start believing it.

Chapter Two

Claudia took her time crossing the busy street, hardly noticing the stares of men in passing cars and ignoring a few catcalls. Long gone were the days when she'd kick a car window or bust a nose over some disrespectful attitude from those with tiny brains and tinier dicks.

The only troublesome matter on her mind now—besides teleporting thieves and snake-eyed Feds—was the perspiration gluing her lace bra and thong to her skin, no matter how many times she pulled at them, manners be damned.

Philly in August was oven-hot, baking the asphalt and concrete and steel. Everyone she passed looked wilted, harassed, and in a damn big hurry to be back inside air-conditioned offices or cars.

Claudia pointed her remote at her rental car, unlocking it with a chirp. The inside was stifling, and she let out a small huff of annoyance. After she started the car, she flipped the air-conditioning fan to High . . . and noticed the light trembling of her fingers.

She wanted to lay the blame on a breakfast of Twinkies and Pepsi, but getting up close and personal with Mr. FBI Man hadn't helped matters. Scowling, she kicked off her heels, then peeled off her stockings.

The smug bastard was tailing her. He'd all but admitted it, and that was the only explanation for why he'd been so . . . reserved. When Vincent DeLuca was shouting at her, threatening her, or when his dark eyes burned with loathing and fury, she had nothing to worry about. When he was quiet and polite, *that* meant big trouble was brewing.

It was much too hot for trouble. *Any* kind of trouble. Why didn't anyone ever pull art heists in Antarctica, anyway? Antarctica sounded sooo good right now.

After digging through the bags and boxes scattered along the backseat, she retrieved a bottle of water and her work clothes. Not caring who might be watching, she wiggled out of her tight skirt and into a pair of shorts. She unbuttoned the suit coat with a sigh of relief and tossed it into the back. As she pulled a T-shirt over her head, tires squealed close by, followed by furious honking.

A woman shouted angrily, and Claudia flipped her off. "Like you never seen boobs before, sister. And I *am* wearing a bra."

It wasn't even see-through, for God's sake. Then she grinned, a sudden thought coming to her. If Vincent was having her watched, she hoped one of his flunkies had gotten an eyeful and reported every salacious little detail to his big, bad boss man. She'd bet a week's vacation that DeLuca would waste no time in giving her shit over it. The man was all too predictable.

Well, he *was* FBI and couldn't help himself, poor thing. His type always came equipped with a self-righteous ego big enough to match any surplus of testosterone. And one look at the man told her he had plenty of testosterone to spare. Back in April, when they'd first crossed swords and territorial boundaries, she'd known he was going to be trouble even before he called her "Sheridan's little bitch."

That had seriously pissed her off. At five nine, she wasn't little, thank you very much—and why did so many men need to call a strong-willed woman a bitch? Vincent had her on the first part, though. Ben Sheridan owned her soul, and she owed him more than she could ever repay.

Thinking back on that first meeting with Vincent, Claudia recalled how his eyes had gone from watchful neutrality to contempt when he recognized her. The average Fed wouldn't have ID'd her, but he was with the FBI's new Art Squad, and they knew all about Avalon. They were competing in the same territory, so she understood the hostility. She didn't even hold it against him, because she knew what *really* chapped Mr. FBI Man's self-righteous ass: Avalon had been at this game for years, and the FBI was still scrambling to match its efficiency.

Those art databases everyone was so proud of? Avalon had one as early as the 1920s and had computerized it a full decade ahead of any others. Then there was the fact that Ben had a wide, international net of contacts. Claudia suspected whoever used Ben as their front man were the ones who actually *knew people*, and they told Ben who to talk to and when. Avalon sometimes struck her as an old, exclusive men's club, but whatever it was, it worked.

Most of the time. Avalon didn't have exclusive bragging rights on bagging bad guys, and they lost almost as many fights as they won. Art thieves were notoriously difficult to catch, and prosecuting them often proved even more difficult.

Claudia drained the last drop from the water bottle and pitched it into the seat beside her. Rummaging through her purse for a hair tie, she kept an eye on the bright red door of Champion and Stone, framed by hanging baskets of colorful petunias, and wondered how long Vincent would stay inside.

God, she wanted a look at the security camera data, but he'd only laugh in her face if she asked. Dealing with the FBI was such a pain in the ass. Too bad the local cops weren't entirely handling this theft. She could work a local cop angle to her advantage, even if it took a little time and patience, but not the FBI.

The security data for this one was probably a lost cause. The best she could do now was wheedle or trick some shred of information about its contents out of Vincent. Hell, even a shred would be better than what she had.

Ben was getting impatient at her lack of progress with the series of thefts; she could tell by how his questions and their conversations kept getting shorter. Claudia hadn't been the least surprised to find that under her boss's classy cool bubbled a temper, a temper she respected and was careful not to trigger.

Too bad she couldn't show the same restraint with Vincent DeLuca. Recalling the look on his face when she'd run her finger down his tie, she laughed softly. The man was a jerk, but damn, he was fine. Still, best to keep her focus on what she was getting paid to do.

Since Vincent most likely knew she was waiting, and was deliberately making her sweat it out, she might as well put the time to good use. She pulled her PDA out of her purse and reviewed her notes, adding details from this morning's theft. Nine confirmed hits, all on the East Coast: New York, South Carolina, Massachusetts, Virginia, Maryland, and the first theft in Philadelphia back in April at the Alliance Gallery. Nothing for weeks, and now Philly again.

Random, except for these most recent three within the Philadelphia and Baltimore areas. The items taken had nothing in common beyond having been replaced by cheap replicas to delay discovery. So far, the thieves had made off with a colonial sampler, a rare atlas, several small paintings, a Japanese mask, a pair of nineteenth-century dueling pistols, a collection of Civil War–era photograph negatives, a French medieval chalice, and now a Greek Corinthian helmet.

If someone was trying to make money by supplying for a select clientele, then a few of these items should've surfaced by now. Thieves were usually greedier than they were smart, and not known for their patience.

Maybe sending the law dogs running around in circles was a deliberate plan rather than sheer luck. If so, the plan was working. Telling Ben she expected the next heist to occur on the east or southeast coast wouldn't earn her any bonus pay.

She turned on the car radio, searching stations until she found a Nelly Furtado song she liked, then sat back, tapping her fingers on the steering wheel to the beat.

Not all art thieves were greedy, unimaginative, or spur-of-the-moment types. Some were eccentric, some brilliant, and a daring few—like Rainert von Lahr—even played games with the authorities. Several Art Squad agents were headquartered in Philly, so maybe the last three hits *were* an intentional slap in the FBI's face. That might explain why Vincent was more bad-tempered than usual.

"And if it isn't the devil himself," Claudia murmured as the door of Champion and Stone swung open and a familiar figure stepped outside: six feet of edgy, dark-haired, dark-eyed, black-suited male aggression, framed by little pink petunias. The whimsical contrast made her smile, even more so because he was completely unaware of it.

He shrugged out of his suit coat, holding it and his briefcase in one hand while he tugged his tie loose and undid the upper buttons of his shirt. By the time he reached the sidewalk's edge, he'd pushed up his sleeves, displaying strong forearms with a dusting of dark hair and the prominent veins of a man with a lean, mean build who worked out regularly.

Sexy as hell . . . The heat low in her belly didn't lie, no matter how much she wished she could pretend she didn't want to corner that man in a dark room, shove him up against a wall, and explore every inch of him. Preferably every hot, slick, *naked* inch of him.

The way he dressed always reminded her of grainy black-and-white news footage from the 1960s, and she'd come to think of the look as Mission Control Cool: slim black suit, white button-down shirt, and skinny black tie. Nothing about this man indicated he was the type who would pay attention to style, yet he must've made a conscious effort with his looks. Did anyone even sell ties like that anymore?

All thoughts froze as Vincent stepped off the curb toward her, grinning.

Oh, shit.

Showing that much tooth meant he was up to no good—or else he finally had enough evidence to break the case wide open. To keep her anger and frustration from showing, Claudia waggled her fingers and grinned back.

Did he have something? God, she hoped not. More than likely he only wanted her to think he did, in order to throw her off or panic her into doing something reckless.

Exactly the kind of dirty trick *she'd* try.

Vincent jogged across the street, adroitly avoiding the traffic. Her heart pounded with every footfall, as much from anticipation of a duel of insults as from purely feminine appreciation of a magnificent male animal moving directly into her target zone.

Resting his hands on the car, he leaned down and grinned. The bare forearms were even sexier up close, and the perspiration-dampened white cotton emphasized the long, lean line of his chest. A feathering of hair was visible where he'd unfastened the buttons over his undershirt, and Claudia unabashedly admired the view. The man had a very sexy neck, one that practically begged her to run her tongue up its salty, warm length to his jaw, and then kiss her way back down to that hollow between his collarbones.

Vincent hadn't missed the quick survey—which she'd made no attempt to hide—and that toothy, predatory grin widened. Oh, yeah . . . dark, disheveled men with persistent five-o'clock shadows and broody eyes made her weak in the belly. But she'd be damned if they'd make her weak in the head, too.

Vincent rapped his knuckles against the window, interrupting her reverie. Claudia hesitated, then lowered it. "What?"

"My people tell me you stripped down in your car."

Hearing him verify that he was watching her somehow made it more . . . stimulating. "Disappointed to hear that I'm not carrying concealed?" As his brow arched, she couldn't resist adding, "Or are you just sorry you missed the show?"

"Is that what you think?"

"I could always arrange for a private showing, Special Agent DeLuca."

His grin faltered, signaling she'd scored a hit.

"You do that again," he said mildly, "and I'll have the locals take you in for indecent exposure. I warned you, Ms. Cruz. And you know there's nothing I'd like more than to toss your interfering ass in jail."

Excitement sizzled head to toe and she flicked her tongue over her lips, pleased beyond all civilized decency when his gaze briefly dropped to watch. No matter what words he said, what he wanted wasn't her ass in jail but in his bed. Or against any reasonably stable surface.

"Always so serious. All work, no play—"

"You want to play, Ms. Cruz?" A breeze drifted inside her car, bringing with it the smell of city traffic, hot asphalt . . . and *him*. He didn't wear cologne, but the scent of soap, perspiration, and warm skin was heady enough. She shifted restlessly on the seat.

"Do *you?*" She matched his cool tone. "Because I don't play so nice."

His smile faded, lips settling into a thin, grim line. "Neither do I—although I won't corner you in an alley and shoot you in the back."

That he'd sink so low as to bring up ancient history irritated her, but defending herself, or pointing out he shouldn't believe everything the media chose to report, would be useless. He'd made up his mind about her months ago.

"And that's *exactly* why your people always lose and why my people always win," Claudia said flatly. "You're just not mean enough."

The window let out a low, electric hum as she raised it, shutting him down before he could respond. Not that it looked like he would; he only glared at her, the sinews of his forearms and neck tight with the effort to control his anger. She tracked him as he stalked away, and pulled out into traffic once he'd turned the corner.

Mr. FBI Man wanted to play rough, did he?

"Gloves are off, *cabrón*," Claudia said softly. "You asked for it, you got it."

Vincent spent the remainder of his day at the Arch Street field office, drinking coffee and chewing pen caps

as he went over the case notes, photographs, and surveillance data. Nothing stood out in the Champion and
Stone camera feed, but it had been a long day and he
was tired and restless . . . best go over them again later.

He'd made numerous calls to other detectives and
agents working the cases, and by the time he'd emailed
a brief update to his supervisor and called it quits, his
mood had deteriorated from bad to worse.

Despite reams of reports, tons of files and photos,
massive megabytes of recorded data, and the combined
brainpower of experienced detectives and the FBI, he
still had *nothing*. When he stepped outside, he irritably scrubbed his palms over his tired, stinging eyes and
swore under his breath as the heat hit, thick with humidity.

He needed a shower and a beer—and sex, considering his lingering reaction to the morning's run-in with
Claudia Cruz—but the chances of getting the first two
were a hell of a lot better than the likelihood of getting
the last one. His sex life was in a sorry state when it
was easier to score a cold, satisfying beer than a hot,
satisfying woman.

Traffic on 676 was slow despite the hour, and Vincent paid minimal attention to the radio news as
he mulled over this case. Once off the highway, he
stopped at a small market to pick up beer, frozen pizza,
and a package of chips, then drove home through quiet
streets lined with trees and brown brick houses.

He lived in an older part of town, an ethnically mixed, middle-class neighborhood that was mostly empty between 6:00 AM and 6:00 PM. Now lights and TV screens glowed behind curtains and blinds, and his neighbors were out jogging or walking dogs. Vincent drove with the windows down, clearing the office stuffiness from his head, and over the sounds of crickets, car engines, and barking dogs, he could hear children laughing.

It lifted his mood, and he waved to his neighbor as he pulled into his driveway. The flare of headlights showed how badly his grass needed mowing and that his sorry-ass flower garden needed watering. A red rubber ball was wedged in the bushes by the porch, which meant the kids had been using his yard as a soccer field again.

"Hey, Vinnie!"

He turned, shutting the car door with his heel, plastic grocery bag and six-pack in one hand, briefcase and suit coat in the other. Jennie was an attractive divorcée in her forties, and she waved at him from where she sat on her porch steps, smoking a cigarette and temporarily escaping her four hyperactive sons.

Vincent suspected she wouldn't mind getting a little friendlier with him, but as much as he liked her, the consequences of sleeping with a woman who had four fatherless boys kept him well out of her range. "How's it going, Jennie?"

"Ain't melted yet. And you? Catch any terrorists today?"

She knew he chased art thieves, but she liked to tease him about it. He couldn't really blame her; chasing terrorists sounded a hell of a lot more glamorous. "Nope, no terrorists in downtown Philly, unless you count taxi drivers. It was a quiet day."

Her laugh followed him inside his house, and he sighed with relief at the cooler air. He took a quick shower while the pizza cooked and the beer chilled to perfection in the freezer, and by the time he'd shaved and pulled on a pair of shorts and a T-shirt, dinner was done.

Vincent clicked on the TV, flopped back onto the couch, and grabbed a slice of pizza. As he opened his mouth to take a bite, his cell phone went off. Scowling, he searched for it under the pile of mail and newspapers on the coffee table. "Yeah?"

"Vinnie, it's me. Steve."

The agent he'd assigned to follow Claudia Cruz. "What's up?"

"Not much. Just checking in."

"Where's Cruz?"

"Sitting in her car, down the street from your place."

What the hell? This was a new tactic for her. Vincent headed to the living room window and separated the slats of the venetian blinds, peering out. Through the trees and bushes, street signs and fire hydrants, he glimpsed a familiar sporty Pontiac rental, the fading light shining along its white paint. "I see her."

"She followed you home," Steve added, unnecessarily.

A tail that he'd failed to notice. Then again, he hadn't expected her to follow *him.* The day's itchy, restless anger flared, and he snapped, "Jesus Christ! Isn't anyone trying to catch the bad guys here? You follow her, she follows me, and I'm—"

Drinking beer and eating pizza.

Anger ebbed, leaving behind guilt. But it was stupid to feel guilty about taking the time to eat a home-cooked meal—or as home-cooked as it ever got, these days. Maybe he should've listened to his mother and gone into teaching. Little kids terrified him, but the older ones weren't so bad.

"You want me to get rid of her, Vinnie?"

"No."

He tried locating Claudia inside the car but couldn't get a clear view. Then, a sudden, unpleasant thought came to him. "Have you seen any movement in the car?"

"Yeah."

"You're sure?"

A pause. "Uh . . . there's a lot of branches in the way, but I'd see her if she got out of the car."

Vincent let the slats drop back into place. "And you can't clearly see the passenger side, can you?"

"No." Again, a brief silence. "Is something wrong?"

"We'll find out. Meet me by her car."

Vincent disconnected, cast a regretful look at his beer, making a small puddle of condensation beside his congealing pizza, and then walked outside.

Before he even reached Claudia's car, he knew she was gone. Steve was waiting for him, looking both incredulous and angry as he began to explain.

Holding up a hand, Vincent said, "She knew you'd assume she was here to watch me. If I'd been you, I would've made the same mistake."

"So she parked here to distract us and took off?" Agent Steve Auckland was a stocky man with a florid face; pale eyes; thinning, reddish hair; and a thick neck. He looked every inch the ex–college football star.

"Exactly."

"She ditched us," Steve said, flatly. "What the fuck? Where's she going?"

"Beats me, but she'll have to come back for the car." Vincent tried the door and wasn't surprised to find it open. After all, she'd parked in a nice neighborhood and across the street from an FBI agent. She'd even left the keys tucked under the visor.

An invitation? Even if not intended as such, it was one now.

"You can call it a night," he said, glancing back at Steve. "Go on home. I'll wait for her to get back."

"You sure?"

"Yeah. Live and learn. We'll know better next time."

Vincent waited until Steve's black SUV drove away before he locked Claudia's car and took the keys back inside with him. Hours passed as he finished his dinner, then worked on his laptop while cable news played out in the background, and through it all he waited for her to ring his doorbell.

After the night turned pitch black, he grabbed his cell phone and her car keys, then crossed the now-quiet street, listening to the buzzing of insects as they circled the lamppost and still feeling the day's heat in the air.

As he unlocked Claudia's rental car and sat inside to wait, something like unease hovered on the edge of his thoughts, though he tried to avoid facing it directly.

She was a big girl, and one who'd ended her career with the Dallas police department after shooting an unarmed man in the back.

Hell, yes, she could take care of herself.

Chapter Three

The apartment lock clicked, then the door creaked as it swung open.

About damn time, too. After hours in this aromatic pigsty, Claudia's eyes were accustomed to the darkness, and she raised her gun, aiming with a steady, two-handed grip at the stocky figure illuminated in the doorway by the hallway lights.

"Don't move. I'm armed and bored outta my mind from waiting for you to haul your sorry ass home, Digger Brody."

Brody couldn't see her, but even his reptilian brain knew when to freeze. Then he snapped, "Who the fuck—"

"I'm not the cops. I'm not here to cause trouble," Claudia interrupted. "I just have a few questions to ask, and I can make it worth your time to answer them. Now shut the door . . . slowly."

"Yeah?" He slammed the door shut instead. "Worth my time in what way?"

Maybe it wouldn't be so bad if Brody gave her trouble. Her mood had been ugly *before* waiting hours for a guy who might not even be of any use to her, and she needed to work out the snarling tension that had been snapping at her heels all day.

But she couldn't afford the trouble, she reminded herself. "In the way your kind likes best, Brody, so lose the sleaze. Keep your hands where I can see them, and don't turn on the light."

"How do I know you got a gun if I can't—"

Claudia fired, the silencer making a muffled, metallic sound. The bullet hit the wall above his head, and he flinched, letting loose a stream of curses as white plaster dust showered down.

"Believe me now?"

She could sense his red-hot rage from across the small room, but he raised his hands and didn't turn on the light. "Who the fuck are you?"

"Nobody interested in your personal affairs. What you do to keep yourself in such fine comforts is between you and the Philadelphia cops, not me."

"I don't know what you're talkin' about. I got no problem with the—"

"You fence stolen property for the mob, Brody. I've been asking questions, and your name keeps coming up regarding the kind of property I'm interested in. I need information about the theft at Champion and Stone, and the one a few months back at the Alliance Gallery."

"I don't move that kind of shit."

"Let's not get off to a bad start with lies."

The scent of Brody's sweat wafted her way on air-conditioned currents—an air conditioner that rattled and wheezed like it smoked two packs a day. She wanted the lights off to keep Brody from seeing her face, but she also didn't want to look at the piles of fuzzy dishes and trash.

"I don't know who hit those two places. It wasn't local business," Brody said, his voice heavy with sarcasm and resentment. "So how come you want to know? And what's in it for me if I talk with you? Not promising you answers, understand, but I'm willing to listen to what you got to offer."

Back in the day, when she'd worn the badge, she'd have gladly taken down a bottom-feeder like Brody. But those days were over and done. "I hear you had some buddies working over a crack dealer in that part of town, and that they saw something."

"Maybe they did."

He hadn't moved and kept his arms in the air as she'd ordered, but she still didn't trust him. The man looked like he could wrestle a bull and win. She kept the gun aimed at the center of his chest.

"Let's cut to the chase," Claudia said flatly. "A thousand dollars for what your friends saw last night, and there's more where that comes from if you keep me informed and play nice."

A brief silence. "Five."

"Brody, don't make me shoot you outta pure irritation." Good. She had his attention. "A thousand's all I got on me at the moment."

Even without being able to see him, she knew what he was thinking. He wanted to take her out and grab the money, but a healthy respect for her gun kept him from making a move. There was also the greed: why settle for a grand if he had a chance to con more out of her? It was a game, and they both knew how it worked.

"If you ain't the cops, who are you?"

"You could say I'm working for someone with a lot of money. So did these friends of yours see anything or not?"

Greed won out, as she'd expected, and he answered, "Nothing that will help you much, just some chick in the back alley by the Dumpster. She was carrying a box. Probably worked for the cleaning crew."

"What did this woman look like? How big was the box? Did she leave in a vehicle?"

"How should I know? I wasn't there."

Claudia sighed loudly. "Little Otis told me you were, so we can cut the 'friends' shit now, too."

"Little Otis?" Brody laughed softly. "I don't believe it."

"He only needed a little extra persuasion to talk." Of

the monetary sort, but she let Brody assume the worst of her.

"You serious?" Brody demanded, his tone incredulous. "You beat him up?"

"There's a reason they call the man 'little.' Answer my question."

"And if I change my mind cuz I don' like how you treat my associates?"

Associates? A high and mighty word for such low-life bastards. She almost snorted, trying to hold back a laugh. "Your loss. I take my money and walk out the door."

"You gonna shoot me then?" Now the tone turned mocking.

Claudia held on to her temper. "As much as I'd like to, no. I told you, I'm not here to mess with your personal business. I just want answers. The offer still stands, Brody, but not for much longer."

Silence followed as he mulled it over, drawing out the silence as long as he dared. "Okay, but you gotta understand I was, uh, busy and not paying a lot of attention. She was young; average build; short, dark hair; and she had on black pants and a shirt. I didn't wait around to see if she got in a car, called a cab, or hopped on a bus or the train. The box was . . . I dunno, box-sized. Not real small, but not real big, either."

"Did she look like a homeless person?"

"Nope. Clean and pretty."

"You could see that at three in the morning?"

"There's a light at the back, by the Dumpster. Just a quick look, but I could tell she was clean. She was wearing lipstick. Glossy stuff."

"All right. Now what have you heard about the Alliance Gallery theft?"

"Like I said, whoever pulled that job wasn't local business."

She couldn't say for sure if he was telling the truth. Looking him straight in the eyes in full light might've helped, if he wasn't a pathological liar. Still, she finally had something more than guesses to work with—and something she hadn't expected. Males usually way outnumbered females when it came to stealing and fencing.

"Fair enough. You gave answers, so I'll pay up. Sit over there by the sink and keep your hands on your head."

"I got no gun on me."

"Don't insult my intelligence. Now move."

He did, but toward her. Expecting it, Claudia swore and ducked. Brody moved fast for a man of his bulk, and his shoulder caught her a glancing blow, rocking her back against the wall. She dropped when he came at her again, his hand snaking toward her gun.

"Stop!" She aimed at his face. *"I will shoot."*

Maybe it was the cold, flat tone of her voice—or knowing it wouldn't matter much to the cops if they found one more body shot full of holes in North

Philly—but he went still, then raised his hands. "Had to try."

"Back off. Now. And keep your hands up." When he'd stepped out of reach, she ordered, "Stop."

"You gonna shoot me?" he asked again, this time with a cold, eerie calmness that matched her own.

"You ever hurt the helpless, Brody? Women? Little kids or old people?"

"No." His lip curled, as if offended. "That ain't my style."

"Good," Claudia said softly. "Then I won't kill you tonight. Take off your belt."

"Hey, hey, girl, you want me as bad as that, and I—"

Claudia fired, then raised her voice over his curses and said, "You know, the first time I shot and killed a man, it bothered me. Second time, not so much. Now I don't even lose any sleep over it."

After letting the threat sink in, she said, "Take off your belt and wrap it around your ankles, good and tight. Then roll over and put your hands behind your head, fingers laced. You know the routine, I'm sure."

When he did as she ordered, she approached, gun steady, rammed her knee and gun into his back, then secured his hands with a plastic tie. She rolled him to his back, moving her knee and the gun to his chest, and pulled out the wallet chained to her belt. After peeling off a wad of cash, she tucked the bills into his waistband.

"Can't say I don't keep my word. A thousand dollars, Brody, and here's my business card." She slipped the card into the pocket of his jeans. "If you hear anything more, call me. Leave a message if I don't answer. I'll get back to you."

"Bitch," he muttered, gasping a little as she lifted her knee from his diaphragm. "Ugly-ass cunt."

Claudia sighed. "That's the first time any man's ever talked trash to me after I stuffed money down his pants. What's a lady gotta do to get a little respect, huh?" She pressed the thick, heavy sole of her shoe over his groin, hearing air rasp through his teeth as he sucked in his breath, his body going rigid. "Well, yeah, there's always that consolation prize of soul-suckin' terror. Don't try to follow me, homeboy. Not in such a good mood today."

Vincent stretched his stiff limbs as best he could, then glanced at his watch and grimaced. He was crazy as hell, sitting in a car and waiting for a woman he didn't even like. He'd already had to explain himself to one patrol cop; he didn't need to do it again.

"Fuck this," he muttered.

Claudia had probably gone back to her hotel, laughing at him all the way. Whatever he had to say to her could wait for when she finally came hassling him for her keys. He swung out of the car, and as he started to lock the door, a noise caught his attention. He tipped his head, listening. Definitely footsteps coming his way, and at this time of night in this neighborhood, who else could it be?

A moment later, a figure emerged from the shadows: tall, long legs, curves in all the right places. She wore jeans, a dark, belly button–baring T-shirt, and a sleeveless denim vest that brushed her hips. Not her usual style; even if it had been the middle of January, he'd expect more skin.

"Claudia."

"Vincent. How sweet of you to wait up for me like an overprotective daddy."

Not the comparison he'd have chosen, considering his usual reaction to her. "Philly's a rough town. Not too smart to walk around by yourself this late."

She came to a stop in front of him in the pale glow of a streetlight, and despite the sticky heat of a summer night, she looked beautiful. A puff of breeze caught a wisp of hair on the side of her mouth, and he almost reached up to brush it away.

"Were you worried about me?"

That mouth curved in a smile, and Vincent met her gaze. He considered denying it, but his pride got the best of him, and he said instead, "I don't like you, but I don't want to see you hurt while you're out trying to get a leg up on me."

Surprise flashed across her face, quickly suppressed—but not quickly enough. He waited for a bitchy comeback, a sly dig. After a few uncomfortable seconds passed, he prompted, "Well, did you?"

"Did I what?"

Was he hearing things, or did she actually sound . . . subdued? "Get a leg up on me." The instant the words left his mouth, he realized they were the wrong choice.

Claudia grinned, her gaze dropping down his T-shirt to his khaki cargo shorts. "If I got a leg up on you, De-Luca, you wouldn't have to ask. You'd know."

"That's not what I meant."

"No, but you'd like to know what it's like, wouldn't you?"

The darkness—and the duskier skin of his Italian heritage—hid the color flooding his face. "Would it fuckin' kill you to just answer me straight for once? Did you turn up anything or not?"

She arched an eyebrow at his dodge, her expression far too smug. "We could go inside your house and discuss it."

Vincent laughed, which surprised her almost as much as it surprised him, judging by how her eyes briefly widened. "I don't think so."

"Aw, and it's such a nice house, too. A testament to the great American dream."

He couldn't tell if she was mocking him or being sincere, but he thanked her curtly, thinking that his mother and grandmother would've approved of his politeness under fire.

"I guess you don't trust me, huh?"

"No, I don't," Vincent said drily. "And I especially don't trust you not to leave behind an unwelcome accessory the second my back is turned."

"That would be rude of me, but I'm sure you'd handle the matter. You're a smart guy, even if you got no sense of humor." Her gaze lowered again. "Though you do casual a lot better than I expected."

"You're not answering my question."

Claudia shrugged. "Did *you* find anything on those security tapes?"

"Nothing useful." It was the truth, yet vague enough to let her think he might be holding back.

"And if I did find something and you found something but we can't find common ground to share it, then nothing gets accomplished." She moved closer, her heat brushing along the surface of his skin, and the perspiration-smudged mascara made her eyes look larger, darker . . . and tired. "C'mon, work with me here, Vincent. We could solve this together."

The weariness, real or imagined, made him hesitate, then he shook his head. "You're asking me to step too far into the gray. I can't do that."

"Why not?" she asked quietly. "I did, and it's not so hard to dabble on the dark side. The pay's pretty good, too."

"Claudia, I read the case file on the incident in Boston back in April. I read the coroner's report on Kostandin Vulaj's cause of death."

"What's this got to do with—"

"I know you were there," he snapped, cutting her off. "There's no question that Will Tiernay put a few bullets in Vulaj, but the coroner has evidence that Vulaj was also hit twice by a high-powered rifle."

When she said nothing, he repeated, "I know you were there. Jesus Christ, Claudia, how often do you go around killing people?"

"I didn't kill Kostandin Vulaj. Tiernay didn't kill Vulaj," she said, flatly. "Vulaj was killed by a bomb he set himself, and in the process also managed to kill his equally stupid girlfriend."

"But you don't deny that you shot him."

To her credit, she met his gaze straight on. "Vulaj was a little nuts by that point. He had an assault weapon and was firing at my colleague *and* at an innocent woman who, through no fault of her own, got caught up in an ugly mess. That mess was our responsibility to clean up. I'm sure you also know Vulaj had kidnapped and threatened to kill this woman."

"You shot him."

She let out her breath in a huff. "Yes, I shot him—and I aimed to disable, not to kill, which the coroner's evidence should prove. I didn't want him dead, and neither did Tiernay: Vulaj would've been more helpful to us alive. *But* there was the small matter of a shitload of explosives in an old factory, and the fact that Vulaj wasn't going to be taken alive. For the record, I don't get off on putting bullets through living flesh and bone, but sometimes I don't have a choice. You got a problem with that?"

"Yeah, I do have a problem with that kind of armed force being used outside federal and state laws with impunity. You don't get to shoot people, even bad people, and then walk away. I don't get to do that. Cops don't get to do that. Nobody does."

Vincent took in a long breath, then let it out slowly. "When it comes to enforcing laws, there's no gray area for me. You either uphold them or you don't—and if you don't, then you pay the price. If there are any gray areas, it's for the courts to decide. That's their job, not mine."

"You really do have that self-righteous stick shoved up your ass," she said softly, but again, without the bite he'd come to expect.

"Make fun of me all you want. Tell me I'm nothing but a government yes-man or a naïve asshole. It changes nothing. You might think you're doing the right thing, but I *know* I'm doing what's right. I've got the law on my side. What do you have besides Ben Sheridan's dirty money?"

He met her gaze, refusing to feel embarrassed by his beliefs, no matter how out of step they seemed nowadays. Trusting and believing in his sense of right and wrong, of justice and fairness, was the only way he could get by in this crazy, fucked-up world. But she wouldn't understand that.

Claudia stared at him a moment longer, her expression unreadable, then shrugged. "Well, can't say I didn't try to save us both a lot of frustration. In more ways than one."

She gave him a teasing smile and a wink as she brushed past him, adroitly plucking the car keys from his hand, then swung open the door.

The streetlight gleamed on the gun revealed as her sleeveless vest caught on the holster at the small of her back.

"Nice gun," Vincent said. And it was: a no-nonsense 9 mm Beretta in basic black, to match whatever the lady might be wearing.

She glanced back at him impatiently. "I'm licensed."

And no doubt she was—to own the gun. "You licensed to carry concealed firearms within the Commonwealth of Pennsylvania?"

Her impatience sharpened to irritation. "I'm covered."

Not a yes. "Show me your license."

"I only have the owner's permit with me, not the license to carry concealed. I left it at the hotel."

Got you, sweet thing. Vincent grinned, though he suspected it looked more like a sneer. "It's a third-degree felony in Pennsylvania to carry concealed without a valid license. You're under arrest."

Claudia stared at him, then blinked and snarled, *"What?"*

Chapter Four

Tuesday morning, Seattle

"What?" Ben Sheridan stopped dead in front of the large reception desk outside his office, certain he must've misunderstood Shaunda.

"Claudia's in lockup in Philadelphia, Mr. Sheridan. The detention unit, down on—"

"I know where it's located," Ben snapped. "What the hell is she in there for?"

"Carrying concealed."

"Oh, for Chrissake."

He briefly squeezed his eyes shut—so much for his morning getting off to a good start—then took a deep breath as he opened them. He'd never seen his receptionist-bodyguard look this flustered. Dressed as severely as ever, in black pants and a chocolate brown sleeveless shirt that was a shade darker than her skin, every line of her body was rigid with tension.

After he'd barked at her, she probably thought he

was angry with her. He flashed her a reassuring smile, then turned to his other bodyguard, who was also his executive secretary. Ellie was small and wiry, and much tougher than anyone would expect if judging her only by her long blond hair, blue eyes, and penchant for pink.

"Find Ron Levine," Ben ordered. "If he's not in the middle of something demonstrably critical, get his overpriced ass on the first available flight to Philadelphia. I want Cruz back to work today."

"Will do," Ellie said, moving past him to her usual spot behind the desk. "I don't think he's in court for anything this week. If he is stuck in court, should I send in Janet instead?"

Ben nodded. "Transfer whatever funds are necessary to post her bail, then get her licensed to carry concealed. Christ, I can't believe she was so damn careless." Ben leaned against the desk, scowling, and folded his arms across his chest. "Did you get any details on what happened?"

"Not really, sir," Shaunda answered. "She just said to tell you the asshole FBI guy did it."

He rubbed his jaw, hiding a smile as he eyed his still-flustered receptionist. "You've been working with me for six months now. You can call me Ben. And what's the asshole's name?"

Shaunda pushed little round glasses up the bridge of her nose and scanned her notepad. Between the glasses and the hair pulled back into one of those complicated twist things, she looked like a librarian, albeit a tall, elegantly lethal librarian.

After a moment, she said, "Vincent DeLuca."

"Gather everything you can find on him." Ben pushed away from the desk. "And I mean *everything*. I'm in the mood to make this bastard squirm."

Shaunda grinned, her dark eyes gleaming. "It will be my pleasure, Mr. Sheridan."

He didn't ask her again to call him Ben, since "mister" was at least an improvement over "sir." Apparently "casual" wasn't in Shaunda's comfort zone in the workplace, although it was certainly well within Ellie's: she'd always treated him as if he were one of her many brothers.

"That's the team spirit. Nobody messes with my people and gets away with it."

Ben headed into his office. On good days he considered it his home away from home, complete with a foldout sofa bed, kitchenette, and shower down the hall. On his bad days it felt more like a fancy prison.

The headquarters of Sheridan Expeditions occupied a three-story building overlooking Puget Sound, its log cabin style well-suited to an international adventure tour agency. The rustic theme carried through to its interior, from the main floor of the travel agency, to the corporate offices on the second floor, and up to the third-floor private executive suite that was locked down as tight as any vault.

People assumed the stiff security was partly because he was Ross Sheridan's heir, and partly because he was worth plenty in his own right. Ben did nothing to dispel that assumption. But even if he'd been stupid enough to try, no one would believe a man with his background and resources was in charge of a secretive organization of mercenaries who hunted down art thieves, looters, and forgers around the world.

He still had days when he wondered how his life had ended up like this—and where he'd be now if he hadn't begged to go along on an ill-fated fishing trip to Malta twenty years ago.

Ben moved toward the wall of tall windows, hands in his pockets. When the weather cooperated he had a great view of Elliott Bay, but this morning a dense fog blended almost seamlessly with the gray water. This was nothing like the view from his hotel window all those years ago, surrounded by an oppressive Mediterranean heat, nearly blinded by the harsh glare of sunlight off the sea's surface and a blue, cloudless horizon stretching out forever and ever.

"Ben, if anything happens to me or my father . . . can I ask you to promise me something?"

Odd, how some memories held strong while others faded. He could still hear Gareth's voice, as well as his own, brushing off the question with an irritated yes. A few hours later, his life changed forever because of that promise. Three months shy of his eighteenth birthday—Gareth had just turned twenty—and everything went all to hell.

He still didn't know who'd killed Gareth and his father, or why. Initial attempts to find answers resulted in blundering into something he wasn't meant to know about, even if it did shed light on what kind of people would've wanted Arthur Whitlea and his son dead. Later Ben had turned up a tantalizing, if tenuous connection between the Whitleas' disappearance and the unsolved murder of an Italian girl in 1943, but it went nowhere except to alert him that Nazis, murdered Jews, and stolen art were all likely involved.

Stolen art was the key; it always had been, or else he wouldn't be doing what he was doing now. To his surprise, he'd become moderately successful at putting art thieves and forgers out of business, although that cause had been the Whitleas', not his. He'd taken up the gauntlet in honor of their memory, and because it gave him the cover and the connections to track down their killers.

Pushing aside his thoughts, Ben headed for his desk just as Ellie called out from the reception area, "Don't forget you have payroll checks to sign! They're in the red folder."

Payroll was *always* a red folder. After years of signing checks for his company, he hardly needed to be reminded, but he knew better than to take his soured mood out on Ellie.

He sat, then shuffled the various piles of paper on his desk into priorities. Besides payroll, he had to proof a report for his stockholders, write a speech for Wednesday night's fund-raising dinner at a local businessmen's club, call his mother, buy a birthday card for his youngest nephew, and last, but not least, teach an overzealous FBI agent not to interfere where he wasn't wanted.

Just another day in the life of the CEO of Sheridan Expeditions, and Big Dog—if not Top Dog—of Avalon.

Ellie poked her head inside his office. "Ron's on his way to the airport. He'll be in Philadelphia this afternoon and should have Claudia out on bail right away."

"Good. Get a message to him to have Claudia call me as soon as she can, no matter how late." Ben booted up his computer. "Anything else I need to know about? It would *really* improve my mood if someone finally tracked down my favorite German archnemesis."

"Still nothing on von Lahr. It appears he's vanished into thin air. Again."

"Funny how archnemeses have a habit of doing that," Ben said wryly. "Especially *this* one."

After fifteen years of eluding Avalon and numerous international law enforcement agents, Rainert von Lahr—thief and purveyor of the stolen, the looted, and the forged—had made a fine art out of disappearing into thin air, leaving behind nothing but the occasional betrayed lover or corpse.

One of these days, though, von Lahr would make a mistake—take up with the wrong woman, piss off the wrong mobster—and Avalon would be there, waiting.

"Oh! I almost forgot," Ellie exclaimed.

Ben gave a small sigh. "Forgot what?"

"I heard from Will. He's wrapping up the theft in Edinburgh, and all the stolen coins are in the custody of the local constables. When he's done there, he'll be heading to London."

With some exasperation, Ben noted Ellie's smile. Tiernay had that effect on women, even the staunchly committed ones.

"Why the change of plans? His last message said he was going back to Italy."

"Didn't ask." Ellie shrugged. "You told me Will was working on his own these days."

On a very private project; information Ben had shared only with Tiernay, who he hoped would put his ex-detective skills to good use in connecting two dead Englishmen to a dead Italian girl. Tiernay was smart, patient, and thorough, and could be trusted to keep a low profile.

At least most of the time, Ben amended, recalling the near-disaster outside Boston four months ago. Recalling another annoying shortcoming on Tiernay's part, he said, "Be sure to watch his expense reports for any unauthorized extras."

"Of course—but you know it's a game with him.

If he didn't try to slip something by me, I'd be disappointed."

"You're just enabling his bad behavior," Ben said as she headed out the door. "But I give up trying to tell you that."

A minute later, scrolling through his new emails, Ben's lingering smile faded as he recognized a familiar nickname. He clicked on the message, then swore softly.

> *I've met with the other representatives, who continue to express their reservations over your handling of Avalon's resources. I've prepared a dossier of their concerns as well as proposals to restructure the current system of crisis management. I'll send the report by courier. Stand by.*

"What are you doing, siding with those idiots? You know better," Ben muttered. But his anger faded as he glanced over the rest of the message, and the postscript even coaxed out a reluctant half smile:

> *PS: I told you this would happen. I win. You owe me a beer.*

Chapter Five

Tuesday afternoon, Philadelphia

Sprawled back in his desk chair, tie tugged loose and sleeves pushed up, Vincent rewatched the security data from Champion and Stone. Notes, photos, and interviews lay scattered across the desk, with only one small spot cleared for the can of Coke dripping condensation into a ring around its bottom. He yawned as he picked it up, his jaw cracking.

The Claudia situation had resolved very late, and he'd expected to fall asleep the second he hit the sheets. Instead he'd tossed and turned all night, and after he finally did fall asleep, it seemed his alarm had gone off only seconds later. His head felt as if it had been scoured out by a wire brush, and the dull headache did nothing for his concentration.

The camera in his head kept replaying the fury and shock on Claudia's face in an unending loop that added to his guilt. *Not* that he had anything to feel guilty about. Or any reason to feel like an ass.

With a low curse, he refocused on his monitor, although he'd already spent hours watching Arnetta answer phones, work on the computer, make tea, dust cases and shelves, and straighten perfectly straight frames.

Such was the exciting life of an FBI special agent. On days like this, he regretted not joining the ATF. Or even teaching high school. Either one would've guaranteed an occasional moment of sheer terror to keep his adrenaline pumping.

Unlike watching security tapes. Again. And again.

This morning's fun involved taking notes from the moment the first customer arrived at Champion and Stone. It had been a quiet day until late afternoon. The first of those customers arrived at 4:23 PM, and Vincent jotted down a description: male, mid-twenties to mid-thirties, gray suit, short blond hair, with a messenger bag. Arnetta chatted up the guy until a young businesswoman in a tan suit walked in at 4:36 PM, and Vince added her time of entrance and details. An elderly couple came in right on the heels of the businesswoman, at 4:40 PM, and Arnetta hustled to keep track of everyone in the right-before-closing-hour rush.

Unlike Arnetta, Vincent had the advantage of being able to switch between camera feeds to follow the customers through the five small gallery annexes.

He tapped the pen impatiently against his lip as he

noted departure times—the couple left with a ratty-looking old doll that cost as much as his monthly house payment—and his thoughts soon drifted to Claudia again.

What was she thinking about him right now? Nothing flattering, to be sure, and if those old wives' tales were true, his ears should be flaming—and then some.

But he'd proved that his threats weren't empty, so maybe she'd finally stay the hell away from him and his cases. He wouldn't miss trading barbs and insults with her, or the cloying smell of her perfume, the sultry swing of her hips, those legs, that knowing smile . . .

Not good, lying to himself like this. He prided himself on being smarter than that.

"Shit," he muttered, rubbing at the tight ache between his brows.

Since the gallery cleaning crew arrived several hours after closing time, Vincent fast-forwarded to the point where they walked in from the back door. His current theory involved thieves working as employees for a janitorial service or security firm, or masquerading as such. It would be the easiest explanation for how they'd gained access to the buildings without leaving any evidence of a forced entry.

This crew consisted of two people: a thin, older white woman, who looked as if she'd spent too many years smoking, and a young, heavyset Latino. The man mopped floors and emptied trash while the woman cleaned the break room and the small bathroom. They completed their tasks as quickly as possible and departed, leaving behind not even a whiff of suspicious activity.

After that, the gallery's lights dimmed to a bare glow and Vincent sat back with a grunt. He'd watched the end of the feed often enough to know there weren't any further signs of activity until Arnetta arrived the next morning to open for business.

The only useful information so far was a verification that small areas of the gallery, including the display case with the helmet, were not covered by the security cameras. A crucial detail, since there had been inadequate security camera coverage in several of the other thefts.

"Anything yet, Vince?"

Vincent paused the feed as his supervisor came up behind him. Edward Cookson was a tall and distinguished man in his early fifties. Shrugging, Vincent said, "More camera blind spots, which explains why there's no pattern to what's been taken. I just can't figure out how they're getting in and out without leaving any evidence except the decoy fakes."

The decoy at Champion and Stone had been bought from an Internet costume store, paid for with a money order, then sent to a post office box registered to a fake address. The PO box address hadn't been used since.

"We must be missing something obvious."

No shit. "They're planning all this in advance, checking out the galleries and museums, which means they have to be on a camera, somewhere."

"Do you have recordings from every break-in?"

"Mostly, but some only go back a couple days. Two galleries had no security data at all, and I was called in too late to retrieve older data on four of the cases, but I want to go back as far as I can with what I have. I'll need a few extra pairs of eyes for that."

"I'll do what I can." Cookson slipped his hands into his pockets, absently jangling keys and change. "You checked alternate entryways, right? Service doors, windows, basements?"

"We're dealing with small operations here, and there's not a lot of money left over for security." Vincent sat back. "Two galleries could've been accessed by windows, but police turned up no evidence of a forced entry. That little museum in New York had a couple of unsecured entrance points, but no evidence of a break-in, so again a dead end."

Cookson glanced over the Champion and Stone files, and pointed to a photograph. "Did you check that bathroom window?"

Vincent nodded. "The glass and lock were intact. The windowsill and frame were painted over years ago and the window hasn't been opened since, so they didn't use that."

"Hang in there, Vince. You're making progress,

even if it doesn't feel like it yet. What's going on with your other cases?"

As with most government-funded agencies, the Art Squad was overworked and spread thin. Vincent gave Cookson a quick rundown of his work and schedule, including an upcoming trip to Columbia, South Carolina, to meet with a local prosecutor on an interstate insurance fraud he'd wrapped up a few months back. Nothing unusual; most of his time was spent at his desk, in court, or meeting with state AGs.

"Good. Sounds like you've got matters covered." Cookson paused. "There's something else I needed to talk to you about. Let's go to my office."

Sensing that it wasn't going to be good news, Vincent held back a frown as he followed Cookson into his office, which was a mess everywhere except the desk, its neatness an odd oasis amid the clutter.

"Shut the door, Vince," Cookson ordered as he sat, then motioned for him to sit in the chair across from the desk. "I got a call a short while ago from the detention unit."

Vincent knew what was coming but kept his expression blank. "Trouble?"

Cookson leaned back, and well-worn springs squeaked in response. "You were apparently involved last night in an arrest outside your residence."

It wasn't a question, but when Vincent nodded curtly, Cookson let out a small sigh. "And of course we're both well aware of this woman's identity. I recall discussing her at some length with you when she first started nosing around. I warned you then against escalating the tension."

"It was a legitimate bust. She had no permit to carry concealed and—"

"I know what happened, as I've just come off a long conversation with the lady's attorney. Ron Levine is not someone I enjoy speaking with."

"I'm sorry," Vincent said after a moment, not sure how he should respond to his boss's obvious irritation. "Ms. Cruz broke a law and paid the price like any other citizen. Sheridan's money and his hotshot lawyers don't mean anything to me."

"They'll mean plenty if Cruz and Levine bring a lawsuit against you for harassment and abuse of law enforcement privileges. She had the appropriate paperwork at her hotel, a fact she claims to have made clear to you and which you chose to ignore, and now she's out of jail and all charges have been dropped."

"You're shitting me." Vincent straightened from his slouch. "There's no way in hell it's real! She's not a state resident, and I know Pennsylvania has some of the most lax gun laws in the country, but she—"

"A certified permit was produced, rendering the charges against her invalid, except for a failure to carry the proper license on her person. The most you'd get on this one is a fine and a slap on the wrist. Let it go,

Vince," Cookson said in that calm, commanding tone that brooked no argument. "Your time and energy are better spent on catching criminals and staying the hell away from the private contractors."

For an instant, Vincent wasn't sure he heard right, then anger flared. "I understand, sir."

"Look, you're still young, still got that fire in the belly. But I have over twenty years on you, and I've been where you are now. I know how this story plays out."

His tone softening, Cookson added, "Every branch of Ben Sheridan's travel agency, here and abroad, is legitimate. His taxes are paid, audits have turned up nothing irregular, and he's very, very careful. Avalon has been in operation for almost a hundred years, and the bank accounts paying those people were established so long ago that they're buried for good. You'll never find a trail. You can't touch this man."

"So I just roll over? Let her do whatever she wants?"

"No, I'm telling you that whatever you do is just an annoyance to Sheridan, so stop going out of your way to harass this woman. In the end she's more useful to us than not, so work with her, ignore her, take her out for dinner, or even to bed if that's what it takes to get her out of your system. I don't care."

Stunned, Vincent opened his mouth to deny any such intent, but Cookson held up his hand to silence him. "I know what she looks like, Vince, so I can't blame you for letting her get to you. But you're being paid to recover stolen art and prosecute thieves—nothing more and nothing less."

"She was carrying an automatic with a suppressor. A few years ago she shot a man to death, four bullets through the back. And you know what happened in Boston just a few months ago. We don't need people like her running unchecked on the streets."

"She killed an escaped felon who raped old ladies and little girls for fun. Nobody cared he was dead, including the police, and it still cost her a career because they didn't like her. The Boston situation was resolved to the satisfaction of the local police. I don't need to remind you there's a lot worse than Claudia Cruz on the streets of Philadelphia." As Vincent began to argue, Cookson held up his hand. "Nor do I need to remind you this matter is not open for discussion."

As far as reprimands went, it was mild but clear, and Vincent could only nod in acknowledgment. He returned to his desk, sitting quietly until he had his temper back under control.

Once he'd calmed down and thought it over, he couldn't deny Cookson was right; this thing with Claudia *was* affecting his ability to do his job. All it took was a glance at his notes to see one glaring mistake: he'd forgotten to mark the departure time of one of the late afternoon customers.

"Dammit," he said with a sigh, irritated at his sloppiness and knowing he'd have to watch the data feeds again. Maybe he'd head to the gym after work, grab a sparring partner for a round or two of boxing, and work off the frustration.

Vincent fast-forwarded to the point when the customer in the gray suit appeared, then focused only on the activity on the monitor. Twirling his pen, shifting restlessly, he waited for Gray Suit to leave. As the minutes ticked by, Vincent switched between feeds, frowning, until he realized he hadn't made a mistake.

The guy in the gray suit had never left the gallery.

"God, I hate jails. They stink and the food sucks. When I get back to the hotel, I'm taking a long, hot shower and then I'm going to eat at the most expensive restaurant I can find."

"The *first* thing you'll do is check to make sure DeLuca doesn't have any surveillance devices in the room. Ben seems to think he shouldn't be trusted to play by the rules."

Claudia glanced at the man sharing the backseat of a taxi with her. In his late forties, tall and dark, Ron Levine was good-looking—if a girl went for soulless lawyers with strong, angular features and coldly assessing eyes.

And those eyes told her he was utterly serious. Claudia started laughing, then couldn't stop, even when Levine shot her an impatient, questioning glare. When she finally caught her breath, she gasped, "Oh, please. You obviously don't know DeLuca. That man's never met a rule he hasn't vowed to obey with every breath in his body."

"Maybe." Levine sounded doubtful. "But you might be that one exception."

Claudia heeded the warning in the attorney's tone. "I'm sorry you had to come all the way here to bail my ass outta lockup." She hesitated. "Was Ben mad?"

"Not particularly, but make sure you're more circumspect with your equipment in the future. The actual paperwork you need is forthcoming, but don't lose the envelope I gave you. I have your pistol in my briefcase. Your suppressor was confiscated. I'm not sure if we'll be able to get it back."

Claudia shrugged. "No matter. I'll ask Ellie for another one. Are you staying in town for the night or catching a later flight back to Seattle?"

"I'll be here overnight to make sure there are no late-developing complications. I'm not anticipating any, as I believe I made my point clear to DeLuca's supervisor, again, but I'd rather err on the side of caution."

Claudia grinned, then smacked Levine on his arm, ignoring his frown. "So how about I buy you dinner, huh? It's the least I can do. My hotel's in Old City, and there's lots of great restaurants in the area. You look like the kind of guy who'd go for a sirloin steak served hot, red, and still bleeding."

"Deal," Levine said without hesitation. "I never say no to free food, especially when it's offered by beautiful women."

"That makes you sound desperate," Claudia said teasingly. "Where's the machismo, man? Aren't you supposed to tell me you'll pick up the check?"

Levine arched a brow, amusement warming his eyes. "I'm Jewish. Just living the skinflint cliché."

Claudia relaxed back in her seat. "Wow. I had no idea."

"That I'm Jewish?"

"No, that you had a sense of humor. You almost made a joke."

Levine pretended not to notice, but she spied a tiny smile tugging at one side of his mouth.

Back at her hotel, Claudia showered, then primped while Levine paced inside her room. She grimaced and made a mental note to steer him away from anything caffeinated at dinner. Enough already with men who were wound too tight!

Going out with Levine was a means to an end—being with a handsome man in Armani would boost her bruised ego—and she intended to take full advantage of the moment, even if it meant having to civilize Levine first with a few glasses of wine. Whereas Mr. FBI Man would need a tranquilizer dart strong enough to take down a bull elephant before he'd make decent company.

Ugh . . . to hell with DeLuca, no matter how fine he looked even in his plain black suits and strange, skinny ties. The next time they met, she'd have a few choice words for that man. And they *would* meet again. She'd make certain of it.

In the bathroom mirror, Claudia surveyed the results of her efforts. The little black sheath emphasized the curves of her breasts and rear as well as the toned muscles of her arms and legs, while the upswept curls softened her face and did great things for her cheekbones. She'd made liberal use of her bag of Lancôme and looked nothing like a woman who'd spent most of the day in jail.

Puckering up glossy, dark red lips, she air-kissed her reflection.

Not bad at all, for a dirt-poor girl whose parents had slipped across the border so their baby could be born in the land of plenty, automatically assuring she'd get at least a shot at achieving that Great American Dream. She'd come a long way from the *barrio*, and once out of it had never looked back.

Not until disaster struck, bringing the stark reminder that nothing mattered more than family, even when she'd betrayed their hopes, their hard work, and all the sacrifices they'd made so she could wear that uniform and badge, and pose for a picture in front of those stars and stripes.

Claudia closed her eyes, then took a long, deep

breath to clear her head. Oh, yeah, nothing like spending hours in jail with a bunch of foulmouthed hookers to bring a girl back to her not-so-pretty roots—and bring all her regrets home to roost with a vengeance.

Levine stopped pacing when she walked out, grinned wolfishly, and said, "Sometimes I really love my job."

"Now *that's* what a girl likes to hear. None of the men I've met so far in this city know how to treat a lady right."

"Their loss."

The interest in those usually chilly eyes lightened her mood a thousandfold, and she flashed her most dazzling smile. "So . . . how about we go find us an obscenely expensive restaurant?"

"Do you want to check on a few things first, as we talked about earlier?"

Ah, the likely nonexistent bugs. The idea that Vincent might bend his rigid principles to such extremes was highly doubtful, but she'd make sure—*after* dinner.

"Later." At his look, she lightly touched his arm and added, "I promise and pinkie-swear."

Levine would assume she was too hungry to do a quick search, but the truth was that if a few Feds really *were* eavesdropping, sweating in a dark, cramped panel van, she had no qualms about making them wait as long as possible.

Tit for tat, boys.

As Levine escorted her out of the hotel, men turned to watch, admiration clear in their eyes. Satisfied, her confidence zooming back to full power, she took Levine's arm and hugged it close to her breasts. She doubted his ego would mind a few extra liberties on her part, and his barely perceptible smile told her she'd guessed correctly.

Hmmm, maybe he wouldn't mind a few other liberties after dinner? Lately, her nights had been awfully long and lonely.

Imagining Levine in her bed didn't trigger the same hot pull of lust as when she imagined Vincent DeLuca naked on her sheets, but Levine hadn't arrested her, either. Reward points in his favor for that!

If Vincent was watching, she wanted him to get a good look at her, wanted him to feel a sharp regret that it wasn't *him* walking beside her on this very fine August night, and he would—

What the hell? Enough of *that*; she'd dressed up tonight to feel good for her own sake, no one else's.

"That's not a very nice smile." Levine's cool, amused voice broke through her thoughts. "What's on your mind?"

Claudia smiled back at him; in her heels, she almost met his eyes on the level. "The truth? That I'd be some pretty hot shit if I could charm even a bloodsucking lawyer like you."

Surprise crossed his face—a look she bet he didn't wear very often—and then he cleared his throat. "This should be an interesting dinner."

* * *

Vincent stood, throwing down his pen as he fought back a whoop of triumph. No need to jump the gun, there might be another reason for Gray Suit not having an obvious departure, and he had to make sure he could account for every conceivable option. First thing tomorrow morning, he'd head back to Champion and Stone for another look around and ask Arnetta if she remembered—

His cell phone rang, and it took him a moment to locate it beneath the paper and files on his desk. "De-Luca."

"Vinnie, it's Steve. She's at her hotel. You told me to call you when she got back."

Despite Cookson's warning, and his own resolve to shake off this woman's hold over him, Vincent asked, "Is she alone?"

"Naw. She's with some guy. Looks like a money-man."

Barely out of jail and already back to business as usual. She was quick, resourceful, and always seemed to land on her feet. He had to give her credit for that. He felt a sharp twist in his gut at hearing she was with a man.

"What do you want me to do now, Vinnie?"

"Go on home. I won't need you to watch her any-more."

"You sure? You said you wanted—"

"I know, but the situation's changed. I owe you a couple beers for all the shit I've had you do these past few weeks."

"Hey, I didn't mind. I needed to work more on my tailing techniques, and she's nice to look at. A lot nicer than a lot of other people I've tailed."

"Ain't that the truth. Tell you what, the next hot babe we gotta follow, your name will be the first on my list."

Steve laughed, and after ending the call Vincent spent the next hour writing up a report, then decided to call it quits. The case hadn't cracked wide open, but he still deserved to celebrate with more than pizza and beer at home.

Hell, he'd go *out* for pizza and beer. Maybe he'd really splurge and order a deluxe burger meal instead of pizza.

The federal building was by the Old City neighborhood, and Vincent headed for Claudia's hotel without even thinking. As soon as he realized what he was doing, he made up his mind to pass the hotel, but then he spotted a parking spot across the street and pulled into it instead.

As the car idled, he stared down at his hands on the steering wheel, white-knuckled with tension. Okay, no regrets for what he'd done last night, not really, but . . . it still bothered him. Arresting her made him feel like a cheat, and when he won, he wanted it to be fair.

Not that she'd give a damn about his reasons or explanations, and everything he knew about Claudia Cruz told him she'd play to win by any means, foul or fair. Still, talking with her seemed like the right thing to do. They'd never had a civil conversation *before* he'd had her arrested though, so what were the chances of having one now?

Vincent climbed out and leaned against the door, tugging his tie loose as the humidity latched onto him like an energy-sucking parasite. While traffic sped past, he observed the lights turning on and off along the nine-storied rectangle of the building, an ever-changing checkerboard of light and dark, with an occasional shadow moving behind the draperies. The window of Claudia's room remained dark.

The FBI had a long history of using whatever means possible to gain necessary information, but he'd handled this situation with Claudia all wrong, and he had to face up to it. It didn't help that she'd willingly opened herself to risk while he'd sat on his ass in his office, complacent in the safety imposed by the long list of rules and regulations he was sworn to obey. Most of the time he didn't bother carrying his gun, since working the Art Squad didn't even involve drama, much less danger.

As Vincent realized that he actually *envied* Claudia Cruz, a taxi pulled up in front of the hotel, and a familiar head of copper-colored hair emerged.

A man followed Claudia out of the taxi. Tall, dark, expensive suit. This would be "the moneyman," probably Sheridan's top-gun lawyer who outsharked the sharks.

The man leaned down and spoke to the cabdriver, then joined Claudia. They talked, and although she touched his arm, laughing, he kept his hands in his pockets.

Vincent grunted, understanding the fear all too well, that if he touched her, it was all over. Adios, self-control.

Claudia suddenly turned and looked right at him. He held her gaze, hating that she'd caught him watching her, yet inexplicably pleased that he had her attention.

She turned back to her companion, a brief, gesture-laden conversation followed, and the man also turned to stare at him.

Damn. This was awkward.

Just as Vincent turned away, Claudia grabbed her companion's tie, yanked him down, and kissed him.

And not a friendly peck on the cheek, or a polite thank-you-for-bailing-me-out-of-jail kiss, either. Vincent could tell it involved tongue, and plenty of it. The man took his hands out of his pockets, grabbed Claudia's hips, and pulled her close.

Aware that this performance was for his benefit, Vincent wasn't sure if he should feel angry or flattered.

They separated after a moment, exchanged a few words, and Claudia walked into the hotel alone. Her companion spoke again to the cabdriver, then started across the street. He took his time, hands back in his pockets: just out for a casual evening stroll. Aside from the mouth and jaw marked with red lipstick, the shirt partially pulled from his pants, and the tie hanging askew, he didn't act like someone who, only moments before, had had his hands full of one hot woman.

Stopping in front of Vincent, he said flatly, "De-Luca."

"Yeah. Who are you?"

"Someone who'd like to talk away from traffic." He cocked his head to one side. "I hear you have a temper, and as I've had a pleasant night, I'd rather it not end in a messy death for either of us."

Vincent stepped back to the sidewalk, and the other man followed. "You're Sheridan's lawyer."

"Ron Levine, and since you already know who I am, let's keep this short."

"My thoughts exactly," Vincent said softly, resenting that smear of lipstick—and his sudden irrational urge to ask the sonofabitch how she'd tasted.

"Stay away from Ms. Cruz."

"I try, but she keeps coming after me." Vincent gave a what's-a-guy-gonna-do? shrug. "So how come I get the lecture and she doesn't?"

"I'm sure you have a reasonable excuse for being

outside her hotel," Levine said, as if he hadn't heard the question. "And I'm sure I don't have to explain the term *restraining order* to you. After all, you are a *law* enforcement agent."

Dick. "Any more words of wisdom?"

"Only a warning, O Zealous One." Levine smiled. "Sheridan is protective of his people. They're family. You don't want to mess with the family."

"The godfather-speak is a nice touch. Nothing like a hot summer night for melodrama."

"I'm giving you the basic facts," Levine answered, not rising to the bait. "If you're as smart as your supervisor claims, you'll pay attention."

Again with the sarcasm.

"Guess she really kissed you good," Vincent said, motioning toward the bright red smear.

Any other man would've instinctively wiped it away; Levine's hands stayed in his pockets. In spite of himself, Vincent admired a self-confidence that rock solid. The man honestly didn't give a damn that he was walking around with lipstick all over his face.

"Yes, she certainly kissed me good." Still wearing that condescending smile, Levine recrossed the street and got into the cab.

Vincent watched until the taxi was lost in traffic, then turned toward the hotel, where a glowing window now marked Claudia's room.

The time for confrontation had arrived, but this

hot-blooded, hot-tempered woman had been sitting in jail most of the day because of him. Charging up to her room might be the movie-style tough guy thing to do, but a real-world smart guy would give her time enough to cool down—and time enough for him to come up with a plan of action that wouldn't end with a knee in his balls.

Chapter Six

Because a promise was a promise, Claudia searched for any bugs and hidden cameras inside her room. Having wired her share of hotels and vehicles, she knew all the tricks—probably better than Vincent, who struck her as less the "stealth" type than the "direct" type.

Then again, he'd been watching her when she came back from dinner with Levine. Maybe she'd read him wrong all along. Or maybe, like anyone, he had his breaking point and she had pushed him too far. Sometimes, she got a little too caught up in the chase and lost sight of the fact that living, breathing, fallible humans were involved.

Her good mood began to fade as she continued her search. It didn't take long, despite her thoroughness. She double-checked and triple-checked, but the room was clean.

She'd begun a fourth round when she realized what

she was doing, and why, and forced herself to stop.

After stripping down to her bra and panties, she flopped onto the bed, reluctant to admit her crazy jumble of emotion boiled down to disappointment that she hadn't found anything. She'd had plans for those recording devices, plans involving lots of sexy groaning and gasping and shouts of "Harder, harder!" and "Oh, God . . . yes, *yes*!"

Stakeouts were boring as hell, and the Feds would probably appreciate a little fun, even at their expense. It would be more fun for *her* if Vincent were eavesdropping, but obviously that wasn't going to happen.

So why had he been outside her hotel? A little zing of delight had gone through her when she spotted him, although seconds later anger had burned the pleasure to ash, and she'd kissed Levine in retaliation. Levine had been most accommodating, and the kiss had been nice. So nice that she shouldn't have been thinking of Vincent DeLuca at all.

Failing to ignore Vincent was bad enough, and now she felt this restless need to see if his car was still parked across the street. Worse yet, she was really, truly disappointed he hadn't bugged her room, even though the possibility had been laughably remote.

So . . . *why* the disappointment?

Claudia closed her eyes with a sigh, guilt sneaking up on her unawares.

Because it was something *she* would've done. Because

it would've brought him down to *her* level. Because it would be so much easier if he fell so low. Because he'd said, *When it comes to enforcing laws, there's no gray area for me.*

It still surprised her, how much those words had hurt.

Every clash with him reminded her of what she'd lost, of those she'd left hurting and disappointed. After what had gone down in Dallas, she didn't even want to try to go back to law enforcement. Maybe some police force would've been desperate enough to take her, but not the FBI. Never in a million years, even if their hands were no cleaner than her own. Except for agents like Vincent DeLuca, who truly lived up to the myth, whom she envied, and whom she so resented because he underscored all her weaknesses and moral frailties.

The last thing she needed was Vincent acting as her conscience, the little angel on her shoulder telling her to shape up, or else.

With a snort of disgust, she sat up. Horny and lonely—always a bad combination, and a few glasses of wine and some heavy-duty kissing had only made the itch harder to ignore. She should have asked Levine up to the room. A night of hard, sweaty sex would've kept her too busy to feel sorry for herself, and Ben's lawyer didn't care about the purity of her morals or the state of her immortal soul.

The sex would have been good, too; she had an eye for that sort of skill. Guys like Ron Levine had to be the best at everything, and all that intensity, restless energy, and pure male arrogance, usually translated to a great lay, if a short-term one.

Wasn't it just her luck that Vincent DeLuca had all that going for him, as well as being honest, incorruptible, dedicated, loyal, and a damn good lawman?

Claudia perched on the edge of the bed, suddenly aware of the generic feel and smell of the place, its impermanence. The darkness and the silence . . . and the isolation.

A sharp knock on the door startled her. She hesitated, wondering who it could be, then grinned. Levine, probably wanting to see if she was playing hard to get.

Lucky for them both, all she wanted right now was a hot man to ride her all through the night and keep her body humming so she didn't have time for moping or brooding.

Halfway to the door, she realized it could also be Vincent. He'd come to the hotel for something—if not to keep her under surveillance, then what? Smile fading, she reached for a T-shirt in her suitcase, then changed her mind. If it was Levine, her being half-naked would save them both the annoyance of awkward small talk. Maybe even foreplay. If it was DeLuca . . .

Narrowing her eyes, Claudia crossed the room,

peered through the door peep, and let out her breath in a soft huff.

Not the man she wanted to see. No, scratch that. *Exactly* the man she wanted to see, but for all the wrong reasons.

Should she ignore him? Let him stew out there in frustration? Call for security? Open the door just wide enough to punch him in the face?

"Claudia, I know you're in there. Open up." The muffled voice sounded tense.

When was he ever anything *but* tense? The man seriously needed a sexual intervention. It would do him a world of good if some woman worked him over until his muscles turned to jelly and reduced his mind to nothing sharper than the fuzz on a baby's head. Hell, it would be a service to humanity.

And what a cause to martyr herself over.

Claudia opened the door as far as the security bar allowed. "What do you want?" she asked calmly, not missing how his eyes widened when he saw what she was wearing. Or not wearing.

After a moment, he managed to drag his gaze up from her bare belly and cleavage, and the heat in those dark eyes sparked a low, sweet tug of desire. Her nipples tingled with the electric charge of his nearness, tightening in response.

"To talk," Vincent said. "I just want to talk."

Like hell he did. He might say that, but his eyes told

a different story. It unsettled her, and even what little she could see of Vincent through the thin opening was too much. Dark, wary eyes with those ridiculously long, thick lashes, the aggressive five-o'clock shadow, a bit of chest hair peeking above the opened shirt and undershirt, that skinny black tie hanging loose. He smelled like summer nights and musky male . . . and beer.

"You've been drinking," she said.

"I meant to come right up, but I had to work up to it first."

She felt a perplexing mix of surprise, amusement, offense . . . and hurt. "The prospect of seeing me is that terrifying, huh?"

"No . . . not exactly." His words, careful and cautious, appeared directed at her breasts. He shifted, clearly uncomfortable, providing her a glimpse of a forearm, all lean muscle dusted with dark hair. The ache of desire tightened, hungering with a will of its own.

How easy it would be to reach out and run a fingernail along the curve of his neck to the hollow at his throat, leaving her mark on him.

She *wanted* to mark him. She wanted to slip off that tie and use it on him in a way that would make that broad, beautiful back arch in a need as powerful as her own.

"I wanted to talk to you about a few things, and I was thinking . . . Shit, Claudia, just let me in. I don't want to do this in a hallway."

Vincent's impatience cut across her thoughts, stirring her instincts of self-preservation and reminding her she couldn't afford to do anything stupid *ever* again.

"Too bad. You're not coming inside, DeLuca, and I don't want to talk to you tonight. Try again when I'm in a better mood."

"Which will be never."

"Probably." She pushed the door closed—or tried to. His shoe blocked it. Annoyed, she looked back up and mockingly asked, "Feeling guilty, are we?"

"No," he snapped, his jaw muscles tightening, before adding evenly, "Not exactly."

"So what *exactly* is this all about?"

He scowled. "Open the goddamn door."

"When nothin' else works, try threats? Trouble is, I don't scare so easy."

Instead of biting back, he suddenly smiled—a slow, sheepish grin that scattered her anger and frustration, and almost melted her resolve. That flash of charm, its unexpected warmth and sweetness, took her completely by surprise. It hadn't occurred to her that he wasn't permanently prickly and difficult . . . that he might actually be a decent guy, if she gave him half a chance.

He wouldn't get that chance tonight. Not if she could hold on to her resolve for another five minutes, anyway.

"A temporary truce," he said, as if sensing her fading resistance. "I swear it."

If he swore a promise, he'd keep it. He was that kind of man. Was a truce what she wanted, though? She was horny, unsettled, weary of rented rooms and lonely beds and all the lies and threats . . . No, no. Letting him past the door would be a *very* bad idea.

"Please?" Again the flash of charm, the hint of warmth. "I feel stupid standing out here. People are staring."

Poor baby. He should've sat through *her* day.

Her wavering resolve hardened. "I said no." At the disappointment in his gaze, she reluctantly added, "Let me sleep on it. If I decide I want to talk to you, I'll be at the lobby bar tomorrow night at ten."

He let out a sigh. "All right. Fair enough."

Fair? Fair would be an apology, but he'd never admit a mistake; she wasn't good enough for that. Claudia waited for him to move his foot, and when he didn't, she stared pointedly down at his shoe. She could still feel his gaze on her, physical as a touch along the curves of her breasts, the length of her belly, the lace of her panties, and all the way down to her bare toes.

Good enough to take to bed, though, the prick. "I want to shut the door."

"Did you know it was me knocking?"

The question caught her off guard, until she realized the intent behind it. "Not until I looked through the peephole."

"You thought it was the lawyer."

"Maybe."

"So the outfit's for my sake. I should've known."

"Really? And how can you be so sure it's not just because I don't care what you think of me?"

"Because I know you."

Hot anger rolled over her—and a little something like fear. Her fingers tightened on the door. "You know nothing about me, DeLuca. Nothing at all. You see what I let you see; you know what I let you know. The rest of it belongs to me."

He'd only ever see the self-confident woman she'd worked so hard and fought so long to become—never that little brown-skinned girl from the wrong side of town, the wrong side of the border, the wrong side of *everything*.

Vincent's eyes narrowed. "I guess that explains why, when you look at me, you only see what you want to see, too."

The instant he stepped back, Claudia slammed the door in his face, closed the security bar, and clicked the lock into place. Retreating to the bed in the safety of darkness, she fell against the mattress, bouncing into its softness. Its vast, empty softness.

God, how had she let him get to her like that? She was a grown woman, a professional, a—

"Ah, shit!" Claudia bolted upright, glancing at the alarm clock. She'd forgotten to call Ben. But it was still early by West Coast time. Besides, the man never seemed to sleep; sometimes she wondered if he was even human.

She dug around in her purse for the cell phone she was using this month and dialed his private number. It rang four times before he answered.

"Sheridan."

"Hi, Ben. It's Claudia."

"It's about time. I spoke with Ron. He said everything went well and you're in the clear."

"Yeah, thanks for that . . . and sorry for the trouble. I really didn't think anything like that would happen."

"Don't worry about DeLuca. I'll take care of him."

Unease prickled. "It's okay. Really. DeLuca's just doing his job. No hard feelings on my end."

After a brief silence, Ben asked, "Any progress in getting to the bottom of these incidents?"

She didn't like the avoidance, though it shouldn't have mattered. Protecting her was Ben Sheridan's job, and it hadn't bothered her before when he'd gone all barbarian on someone else's ass on her behalf.

"Maybe. I talked with a guy who saw a woman outside the Champion and Stone gallery early in the morning, carrying a box. It sounds suspicious enough to check out." She decided against telling him how much she'd paid for that info; it'd go on the expense report, and Ellie would take care of it without a question. "I asked him to contact me if he heard anything else. Other than that, nothing new."

"All right. Keep me posted. I have another assignment for you, so you'll have to fly out of Philadelphia early next week."

"No problem." She was always juggling multiple assignments, but the prospect of a new challenge didn't make her as excited as it usually did. "Just let me know when, so I can wrap up what I need to on this end before I leave."

"You're okay?"

"Yeah, Ben, I'm fine. My ego took a bruising, but that's all."

"Happens to the best of us." He sounded amused, and relaxed. And not for the first time, she wondered how he managed to juggle so much without ever making a mistake. Man *definitely* wasn't human. "Make sure you check in again soon."

"Will do. And again, I'm really sorry. I should've been more careful."

"You'll know better next time."

She considered asking him not to retaliate against Vincent, but she was too tired to deal with the questions Ben would ask.

After ending the call, she tossed the phone on the bed. Ben hadn't sounded angry, only impatient. If she didn't turn up any solid leads soon, he'd have to pull her. Keeping her tied up on a case that had hit a dead end would be a waste when she could be making money for him elsewhere.

Her cell phone rang and she picked up, frowning when she didn't recognize the number. "Hello, who is this?"

"Digger Brody. You the one who wanted to know about the woman outside the gallery, right?"

"Right." Maybe the night wouldn't end as a total waste. Hot damn. "You got something for me, Brody?"

"Yeah. I think you'll want to hear this. It'll cost ya."

"We'll see. Let's meet and talk about it."

After leaving Claudia, Vincent ended up at a bar a few blocks from his house. He wanted the distraction of people in motion, talking, connecting. The white noise of the bar would help shut *her* out. And if he got totally shitfaced, he could just walk home.

"Hey, Vinnie." The cute and plump twenty-something bartender smiled a greeting. "Bad day, huh? That suit looks like's it's been through a lot."

A quick survey proved her right, and he made an effort to straighten his tie and tuck the loose folds of shirt back into his pants.

"Good and bad." Vincent sat on the stool, elbows resting on the bar. "And in that order."

"The usual tonight?"

"Yeah. Thanks, Julie."

She set a cold beer in front of him, its dark, yeasty aroma filling his senses, then moved on to a customer who'd just signaled for a refill. The Leone family owned the place, and their youngest, Joey, sometimes did yard work for Vincent for a little extra cash.

He glanced around, spotting a few familiar faces, then snagged a dish of nuts. Beer and nuts and a soothing darkness were just what he needed to relax, and the smells coming from the kitchen had his stomach growling and his mouth watering. He ordered the biggest burger on the menu along with a basket of fries, and had started seriously working on his beer when a woman sat down beside him.

"Hi. Is it okay if I sit here?"

Vincent smiled back at the pretty bottle blonde in the little, flowery dress. "Yeah, sure."

"I'm Candy."

He held back a wince. Meeting a blonde named Candy in a bar only happened in bad sitcoms. Dutifully, he asked, "Need a drink?"

"No, thanks. I'll take care of that."

Vincent hoped she was just being friendly rather than trying to pick him up. He'd long since learned there was no such thing as no-strings-attached sex, and he wasn't such a bastard—or that hard up for sex— that he'd ease his frustration while pretending she was someone else.

"So . . . you there in the suit. You have a name?"

"It's been a long day. Forgot my manners." He smiled again. "I'm Vincent."

"You look like a man with woman troubles, Vince."

Why did everybody call him Vince or Vinnie, even after he'd introduced himself as Vincent? He preferred Vincent. His mother, alone out of the entire family, had always insisted on calling him by his full name, and the only other person who called him Vincent was Claudia Cruz.

All hail the irony.

"Not exactly." Hearing his answer, and recalling Claudia's exasperated response to his earlier hemming and hawing, he added, "But close enough. Is it that obvious?"

"Only to a woman who's having man troubles."

"Ah, I see." All right; he'd been unfair to hold the bimbo name and bottle-blond thing against her. "Sorry to hear that."

The woman had a great smile, and it added an almost irresistible sparkle to those big blue eyes. "Thanks. It's a bitch when the guy won't even see me because he's too caught up in some other woman." She sighed dramatically. "Same for your situation?"

"Nope. She notices me. She just doesn't like what she sees."

Candy gave him a once-over that left him embarrassed as well as faintly flattered. "Then the lady must be blind."

Not wanting to encourage this line of conversation, because he knew where it would lead, he shrugged and picked up his beer. "It's complicated."

"It always is." Her drink arrived, cranberry juice and vodka, and Vincent was duly impressed when she knocked back most of it in one long swallow. He had to admit, it was seductive. Putting the glass on the bar, she added, "But at least she knows you're alive."

True enough. "Good luck. In getting noticed, I mean."

"Thanks, though I may have to do something dramatic for that to happen."

Vincent didn't envy the poor bastard who'd run afoul of this woman. "That's always one option. Not my style, personally."

She got the hint that he didn't want to talk, and dropped a few bills beside her drink. "I think it's the only option at this point. I should be moving on—big day tomorrow. It was nice talking with you, Vince DeLuca."

His burger and fries arrived, distracting him, and a moment passed before he realized he hadn't told her his last name. Vincent swiveled around, but she'd already left. He surveyed the bar again, seeing only those who knew him as he knew them: by first name only. Then he spotted Joey Leone clearing tables in the back corner.

He caught the boy's attention and waved him over to talk about hiring him for a few hours of yard work—and to confirm that, yes, the woman had quizzed Joey about him. Vincent then devoted himself entirely to his beer and burger, eventually letting his thoughts drift to the security recordings and what they meant . . .

and, inevitably, back to Claudia's generous curves in the black bra and panties; the anger in those usually cool dark eyes, and the smear of lipstick on the lawyer's mouth.

Vincent finished off the beer and ordered another. It had been a long, long day, and it looked like it would be a long, long night, too.

Chapter Seven

"Is that blood on your shirt? Oh, God, are you all right? Are the police after you?"

Rainert von Lahr shut the hotel room door, raising his brow at the barrage of questions from the frantic blonde wearing his T-shirt—and little else. "Yes. Yes. No."

A look of confusion crossed her face. "But . . . wait," she said as he pushed past her. "What happened? Are you in some kind of trouble? Your hand is—"

"Business negotiations. That is all you need to know."

He stripped off his suit coat, shirt, and tie, and threw all of them, along with his keys, cigarettes, and lighter, onto the table by the window. Seeing the small smattering of blood irritated him all over again. That shirt had been one of his favorites. Now it was ruined, and the woman fluttering around him in distress didn't help his mood any, either.

"Are you sure the police—"

"Vanessa, shut up," he snapped, perversely gratified by the flash of fear in her eyes as she backed off.

What had Kostandin Vulaj seen in this frail, neurotic woman? From the moment Rainert had held out his hand to her in Rio, he'd tried to understand why Vulaj had died for her—and why *he'd* not only bothered to help her but also dragged her around with him ever since.

He had enough problems to deal with: his increasingly complicated workload, Avalon hounding him, Vulaj's vengeful kin taxing his patience, his plans to get Ben Sheridan off his back, the Marlowe forgery fiasco that had nearly earned him a knife in the kidneys this morning. The last thing he needed was to babysit a dead partner's ladylove, even if he'd had a certain fondness for Vulaj and felt a twinge of responsibility for the younger man's death. Learning that Vulaj had planned to cheat him hadn't eased that niggling guilt. Maybe because Vulaj was dead and couldn't fight back, but more likely because it had been a neatly ambitious little double cross, one Rainert could appreciate.

It was exactly what he'd have done, back in the day.

After he kicked off his shoes, he looked up to see Vanessa pacing back and forth in the narrow space between the beds, her small breasts jiggling beneath the thin cotton. He took a moment to admire the show, because, despite her many flaws, she did have very nice breasts.

Yes, well, *that* was one reason why he'd taken her with him, but hardly the important one. There were many women more beautiful than Vanessa Sharpton, and she presented him with a multitude of irritations: the jumps and trembles at sudden noises; the frequent sobbing that woke him in the night; the dazed, wounded gaze following him whenever he was with her, as if she thought he could solve all her problems with a magical snap of his fingers; the fear in her eyes whenever he got too close.

He hadn't touched her, and they slept in separate beds, but she was always *there*, sometimes so like a shadow that he forgot her presence, and other times a puzzle he studied with almost clinical fascination.

Aware of his gaze, she self-consciously folded her arms over her breasts and sat down on her bed. "Don't stare at me like that."

"You should relax," Rainert said, for what had to be the hundredth time. "And if you don't want me to stare, then put on some clothes."

She made a fluttery, distressed motion. "I was taking a *nap*. It's not like you ever tell me where you're going or when you're coming back. And of course I'm tense! I lived in London for years . . . what if I run into someone I know?"

"If you do, we'll deal with it." He shrugged. "In the meantime, everybody thinks you're dead, so you might as well enjoy the undead life while you can."

Her eyes widened, full of surprise and confusion. "You're insane."

As Rainert made his way to his bed and sat, he brushed against her. She flinched, and averted her gaze from his bare chest. "I assure you, I'm quite sane."

He examined his knuckles, taking in the swelling, the bruises and cuts. Nothing serious, but the sooner he iced them the better. "I'm not in a good mood at the moment, however, so I'd advise you to calm down and stay quiet."

She glanced at his hand. "You said you were going to give me a chance to get back at those people who killed Kos. So far, all we've done is fly from one country to another. . . . And how do you *do* that? Aren't you afraid of being caught?"

"I have my ways."

She glared at him. "Kos always used to respond to my answers with nonanswers, too. It pissed me off then, and it pisses me off now."

It was these little flashes of backbone that intrigued him most, along with a more recent discovery that, if he angered her enough, she'd fight back. Still, entertainment factor aside, the woman continued to be more trouble than she was worth.

"It's not complicated, Vanessa. Those people, as you call them, are always after me. That won't ever change—not until they catch me or kill me." Fear flashed in her eyes. She was clearly afraid of being stranded again, by yet another man stupid enough to get himself killed. "The trick is to stay one step ahead of them, and doing so is much easier than you'd think."

"Why?"

"To begin with, I don't act like I'm afraid of being recognized, or that I don't have every right to be where I am." Her cheeks flushed pink. "Suspicious behavior is noticed. I also know a lot of people who either owe me favors or want me to owe *them* favors. I keep proving myself more valuable alive than dead, though there are days when I have to remind people of that."

"Is that what happened today?"

He leaned back, absently massaging his knuckles. The ache had progressed to a pounding throb; by tomorrow he wouldn't be able to move his fingers. Fortunately, there was little chance he'd have to shoot anybody in the next few days, and, with any luck, the bruising on his back—where he'd hit the parking lot wall—wouldn't be too much of an inconvenience, either.

"There was a forged manuscript I was asked to recover before it could be used against several long-standing associates of mine. It was partially my fault the forgery was stolen in the first place, so I felt obligated to act. I recovered the manuscript, but a copy had already been made. Probably several. A copy of a fake wasn't strong enough evidence to legally prosecute my associates, but that didn't stop Avalon from going after them. The few that managed to escape are still upset with me, as you can imagine."

"Will these associates come after you again?"

Rainert smiled. "No."

She paled. "Oh."

He went to retrieve the ice bucket from the bathroom. "I need to get more ice. Is there anything you'd like while I'm out? Chocolate? Soda?"

Vanessa shook her head. "No, but thank you."

So polite. So ordinary. So like the kind of girl he'd have brought home to meet his parents in another life and time—and so unlike the majority of women he'd been with over the years since he'd left that old life behind.

He pulled on a clean shirt but didn't bother buttoning it, then padded down the dim, carpeted hallway in his stocking feet. It occurred to him that her boring ordinariness might be another reason he kept her with him: the novelty of her recently-fallen-but-still-a-good-girl appeal. There was also the issue of her being as helpless as a kitten in a kennel of dogs; like any man, he could be flattered into protectiveness.

As he scooped up ice, he wondered if that instinctual need to protect had caused Kos Vulaj's fatal attraction to the woman. It seemed the sort of thing a younger, more emotionally immature man would fall for—the stupid bastard.

Vanessa was still sitting on the bed when he returned, but she'd slipped on a pair of shorts. At least she no longer looked pathetically grateful when he walked through the door, merely relieved. No matter how many times he assured her he wouldn't abandon her, she still didn't trust him.

As soon as the door clicked shut, she headed toward the bathroom, brushing against him as she took the ice bucket from his hands. "I can do this. You go sit down while I grab a towel."

Although he'd had more than his share of experience at self-doctoring over the years, Rainert didn't protest. This was her way of not only thanking him for taking care of her but also of making herself valuable enough that he'd have a reason to keep her around. More important, a reason that didn't involve sexual favors. He knew what she was thinking more often than not; she wasn't a very good liar, and her emotions were ridiculously transparent.

It irritated him that she thought he'd stoop so low as to bother a grieving woman in that way, but he couldn't entirely blame her. It would be stupid of her to assume he was offering his help with no strings attached. She was at least astute enough to know someone like him couldn't afford to operate on such terms.

He sat on his bed and tried to appear as nonthreatening as possible when Vanessa returned with the bucket and several towels, one of which she'd wrapped around a bag of ice cubes. She knelt and took his hand, turning it from side to side, and winced.

"That must hurt." The sympathy in her voice sounded genuine, and for once her touch wasn't hesitant.

"I've had worse."

"You're lucky you didn't break any bones." She paused. "Or at least none of your own."

The towel of ice was merely cool at first, but the chill soon spread and began its job of numbing his knuckles and fingers. The pain kept him occupied enough that he could ignore her nearness. He might have little interest in her sexually, but his body noticed, on a purely primitive level, that she was warm, sweet-smelling, and very female.

"Did you take anything for the pain? I think we have a bottle of ibuprofen in one of the suitcases. I can go look if you'd like."

"Not necessary."

"Keep the towel on like this for a few minutes, then turn it over. The ice should last long enough to start to bring down the swelling. Be careful of the bag, though. I'm not sure it won't leak." Vanessa scooted closer, bending to check the ice, and her hair brushed along the skin of his belly. The neck of her T-shirt gaped as she did so, providing him with a tantalizing glimpse of rounded, bare breasts. When she'd put on the shorts, why hadn't she also put on a bra?

She realized her mistake almost at once. Her gaze

flew upward, and then her cheeks flushed an even darker pink as she hastily stood and backed away.

He didn't bother hiding his amusement. "I appreciate the view. But not the fear—I've already told you I won't touch you unless you ask. I grow tired of you looking at me like I'm going to rape you and then slit your throat. It offends me."

"I'm sorry," she whispered, eyes downcast. "It's only that I don't know if . . . I don't know you at all."

"We've been together for four months. Have I given you any cause to fear me?"

"I don't know you," she repeated in a whisper. "Or what you're capable of. Did you kill someone this morning?"

Shifting the ice and towel, Rainert frowned as he considered how to answer her. "No, but I would have, had it been necessary."

Silence filled the small room, making the scant distance between them feel even greater. "I thought maybe it was like that," she said. "But sometimes you do seem like such a nice, polite man."

"I was raised by very strict, conservative parents." She stared at him, so plainly surprised that he added, irritably, "I do have parents like anyone else."

"I'm sorry, I didn't mean it that way."

"Stop apologizing," he snapped, and immediately felt like an ass. Or worse, since her trembling submissiveness sometimes goaded him to lash out even more.

An unsettling realization, even for someone like him. "Vanessa, sit down." When she did so, eyes still downcast, he added, "I have no illusions about what I am, nor do I make excuses. No stories of childhood woes or any of that. As hard as it is for you to believe, I do this because I want to, and because I'm good at it."

That got her attention. "So one day you simply woke up and decided your life's ambition was to be a common thief?"

Her words stung, as no doubt she intended, but at least her response was preferable to apologies. "It was a gradual process, and I'm far more than a common thief. I'm a businessman with a small, select clientele, filling a very specific need."

Her expression remained skeptical. "So how did you end up as a not-so-common thief? It would be nice if you'd answer at least a few of my questions. I still don't know why we're in London, or how any of what we're doing can be viewed as revenge, or—"

"I told you, we're in London because I have business to attend to. As for revenge, that's part of why we're here as well. A few final arrangements needed to be taken care of, but Avalon should get its first inkling of trouble in about"—he glanced at his watch—"eighteen hours."

Her eyes widened. "What are you going to do?"

"Personally? Nothing. All you need to understand is that I'll do whatever is necessary to survive." Rainert leaned back against the headboard, stuffing the pillows behind him until he was comfortable. "Think of it as a small, quiet war that other people don't know about, and probably wouldn't care about if they did. On each side, every action and reaction has its consequences. For a long time, I believed it was wisest to avoid direct confrontations with Avalon, to accept the losses that came my way, along with the few opportunities to get even. Recently it's become too difficult to continue in this manner. There is also the matter of my responsibility in Kos's death."

"How? You weren't even there and—"

"It doesn't matter. His people believe it was my responsibility, and they are not people I can afford to anger or offend. Consequences, you see? The two of you were stupid and greedy, and now look what has happened. I have very powerful members of both the Albanian and Greek mafia pressuring me for results, you're a wanted fugitive, and Kos is dead. You think it was heroic that he died to give you a chance to escape, but the reality is that he'd have been far more useful to you alive."

"You have no idea what it was like, what had happened . . . he had no choice!"

"I know exactly what he was thinking and the choices he had, but I can't blame him for picking the quick and easy way out. I will never go to prison, either."

"Please don't say that," she said, all color draining from her face.

"I was in the army a long time ago. The Bundeswehr, in my native tongue." He didn't speak German much anymore. Sometimes, he wondered if he would sound like a foreigner to his own family if he ever went back home. "I was trained as a sniper, and I was quite good at it. You know what a sniper does, yes?"

"Yes," she said flatly.

"Then you know I am trained to kill from a distance, in secrecy. When I did this for my country, I was rightly praised. Killing the enemy is acceptable. What I'm engaged in now is merely a different kind of war, and I am still a sniper. Only now, I use different weapons."

Rainert swung off the bed and headed toward the room's small table. He'd bought a decent bottle of scotch the night before, and a bottle of wine for Vanessa, which she hadn't yet touched. "I don't kill needlessly, and, if I can help it, I don't kill outsiders. It draws unwelcome attention."

"*If* you can help it? How often do you kill people? Were any of them just innocent bystanders?"

He poured a glass of scotch before he turned back to her. "There has been . . . collateral damage. I regret it, but cannot undo what has been done."

"Dear God." She looked even paler than before. "Doesn't it bother you at all?"

"Not really. I've long since crossed my Rubicon."

When she continued to stare at him blankly, he sighed and explained, "The Rubicon is a river in Italy, and when Caesar—"

"I know what 'crossing the Rubicon' means," Vanessa snapped.

"My apologies. Most of my associates are the kind of people who wouldn't have."

"Lovely. And at least now you know that I'm not an idiot—just shocked and horrified that I've been sharing a room with a murderer."

"I'm afraid you're in no position to pick your Prince Charming," he said, grinning. "Be happy that I don't generally kill girls."

"I wish I'd died at that miserable factory with Kos."

"But you didn't, so stop whining." He refilled his glass—between the alcohol and the ice pack, the ache was fading—and headed toward the bathroom. "I'm going to take a bath—the morning's negotiations didn't do much for my back, either. By the way, I'm taking you shopping before we leave London."

"No," she said flatly. "I'm not going anywhere that public."

"You'll go where I tell you to go, and you know it." He closed the bathroom door.

"Shopping for what?" she asked.

"You need more clothes. I'm tired of you wearing my undershirts, and you need something pretty. In the right clothes and setting, you'd be attractive enough."

"Why, thank you." Her voice dripped with sarcasm. "Such a flattering compliment."

While he began running the bath, he heard the bed-springs creak as she flung herself down—he *was* getting better at prodding her out of those annoying moods. But no sooner had he relaxed in the hot water, scotch in hand, than he realized he'd forgotten something.

"Vanessa," he called. "Be a good girl and bring me my cigarettes and lighter. They're on the table."

A loud sigh. More bedsprings creaking, then stomping footsteps. Yes indeed, he'd roused a little of her fighting spirit. He'd also pricked her feminine pride, and she'd go shopping with him, if only to prove that he was wrong and she was more than "attractive enough."

The footsteps closed in on the bathroom door. "Are you decent?"

"Haven't been in a very long time," Rainert said, drily. "I'd mock your American prudishness, but you're British, and I believe that's even worse."

"This, coming from a German? Everybody knows Germans are repressed."

"I thought that was the Russians."

"Close enough. Same geographically frigid north."

He couldn't tell if she was trying to get back at him in her own way, or if she truly couldn't handle the sight of a naked man in a bathtub. "So you're saying only the sun-baked Italians, French, and Spaniards get to claim the passionate reputation?"

"And Greeks and Albanians."

Obviously she'd never been in Madrid in August; it was too damn hot for sex. "Vanessa, bring me my fucking cigarettes."

She obeyed, tight-lipped, and slapped the package and lighter down on the bathtub's edge, avoiding looking at him. "It's a filthy habit."

"First you mock my virility and now you nag at me like a wife. How domestic of you," he said coldly.

Instead of hastily retreating, as he'd expected, she sat on the toilet seat.

"What now?" he asked, reaching for the lighter.

"I do think you're a very handsome man."

He stared at her a moment, brow arched, before lighting up. "Why, Vanessa, I'm almost flattered."

"Don't do that . . . I'm serious. I wanted to make it clear that I'm not totally self-absorbed and blinded by my troubles. You have been rather decent to me, all things considered, and I am grateful."

"Is there a point to this? Because I want to sit in my bath and drink and smoke in peace."

"I can't repay you for the trouble you've gone to on my behalf. We both know that. Even though I don't want to have sex with you, if it's the only way I can make good on my debts, I wish you'd simply say so. Stop trying to be nice to me and buying me things, pretending like you care."

Rainert took a long drag, then blew out the smoke

slowly, letting the silence lengthen between them. She shifted uncomfortably, gaze darting toward him but still unable to look directly at him.

"I need a new shirt, and you need new clothes. You also need to get out of this room, which is why I'm going to take you out to dinner after I buy you a pretty dress. That is the extent of my ulterior motives."

"Are you telling me the truth? Really?" she asked after a moment, eyes narrowing. "I know I can be somewhat naïve, but—"

"I don't want to fuck you," he said, as bluntly as he could, and was amazed all over again by how she blushed because he'd offended her good-girl sensibilities. That someone like her had ended up with someone like him boggled the mind. "But if you throw yourself at me in bed tonight, I can't say that I'd kick you out."

"I'm not going to do that."

He sighed. "If you're not going to join me in the bath and share a drink or a smoke, then get out. I need to be alone now."

This time she left, quietly shutting the door behind her.

Women—nothing but trouble. Too bad he couldn't live without them.

Chapter Eight

Vincent arrived at work very early—if he couldn't sleep, he might as well work—and with a few hours to kill before Champion and Stone opened, he loaded the gallery's security data from the day of the investigation. He followed the activity from the moment Arnetta walked through the front door to her discovery of the decoy helmet.

A customer was already waiting when Arnetta arrived: the businesswoman from the day before, who'd lost a watch and came back to look for it in the gallery. He'd already recorded all this in his notes, and he watched as the two women hunted through the rooms, Arnetta even getting on her hands and knees.

On his second viewing, as he switched between feeds, he noticed another woman leaving the gallery and couldn't remember if he'd marked down her arrival time.

Vincent switched over to the front door camera to pinpoint when the second woman had walked into the gallery, but he couldn't find her. What the hell? Unless she'd climbed through a window or slipped in the locked and secured back door, there was no other way inside except through the front—and the camera couldn't have missed her.

As understanding gelled, crystal clear, he muttered, "I'll be damned."

Now he had a fair-haired businessman in a gray suit who'd walked in but never out *and* a brunette in a black skirt and red shirt who'd walked out but never in. It raised an interesting if far-fetched possibility: what if the woman in the red shirt was Gray Suit?

Hell, why not? Nothing in this case made any sense, and thieves often relied on disguises and wigs.

Enthusiasm rejuvenated, Vincent quickly made screen captures of the woman in the red shirt, then hunted through the piles on his desk for the images of Gray Suit that he'd printed yesterday. Security cameras didn't provide the sharpest images, and the woman's face was obscured by her hair. He didn't have a real clear image of Gray Suit, either, but he looked taller than the woman, much taller than an average woman. Nothing hinted that Gray Suit was anything but male, though there wasn't enough clarity to make out any beard stubble.

A man *could* pass for a woman—and vice versa.

Vincent sat back, frowning. This could be a case of one person masquerading as a man and a woman, or it might be a male and female team, maybe even more than two people.

Suddenly he wanted very much to know what Claudia had turned up—if she wasn't just jerking him around.

The time she'd set to meet with him was hours away, and there was no guarantee she'd even show, so he left a message for her at the hotel.

She didn't call back before he left for Champion and Stone. After he talked with Arnetta, he'd spend the rest of the day calling the detectives on all the other cases, sorting through security data for them, and looking for visitors and customers who miraculously appeared and disappeared—and maybe even changed gender.

At two o'clock, Claudia went to meet Digger Brody at Rittenhouse Square, a short distance from her hotel and a very public place, crawling with tourists and local law enforcement. To blend with the tourists and the office worker crowd, she wore a loosely tailored jacket and pants in tan linen with a hot pink shell. Given the heat, a tee and shorts would've been preferable, but it was easier to hide a shoulder harness under a suit jacket. In such a public place, though, Brody would probably make more of an effort to mind his manners.

Since she'd already paid him once, he had a good reason to keep their appointment, but after waiting nearly a half hour she had to admit he was a no-show.

Standing next to the whimsical frog sculpture, hands on hips, Claudia tapped her foot impatiently. Why had Brody passed up the chance to make a little easy money? He wasn't the type to be scared off by crowds, especially since he'd suggested this spot.

Narrowing her eyes behind her sunglasses, Claudia took a closer look around. If he didn't show, it was because either he wasn't able to or he intended to set her up.

Surrounded by so many people, she had no way to tell if anyone was watching her. She tried the call-back number on her cell phone to see if she could raise Brody, but it turned out he'd called from a pay phone.

Irritated and overheated, Claudia headed toward her new rental, keeping alert to any hint of trouble. A drawback to having exhibitionist quirks was that she liked to stand out. She'd chosen her outfit because it wouldn't hinder her if she had to run or duck, but it wasn't totally low-key. A man staring at her could mean he liked how the deep V-neck of the shirt displayed her cleavage, or it could mean he was memorizing her face to shoot her later.

Great. Now all she had to show for her efforts was vague information about a woman sneaking around Champion and Stone's Dumpster at some ungodly hour of the morning, and, worse, she'd paid some loser a grand for it.

If it weren't for her pride, she'd call Ben and ask him to pull her out, leave this freakin' mess to Vincent to sort out.

As she got into her car, she checked her watch. She had hours yet before she met with Vincent—*if* he showed up; maybe it would be her day for men leaving her high and dry—and that worked out perfectly. She wanted to check the layouts at both of the Philly galleries that had been robbed.

As she drove to the Alliance, she kept an eye on her mirrors for any tail that wasn't the black SUV she already knew originated with Vincent, but she didn't spot anything suspicious. Not even the SUV—and what was up with *that*? The SUV had been such a nuisance, and all of a sudden it just stopped?

Midafternoon traffic wasn't much fun, and it took her longer than she'd expected to get to the Alliance Gallery. First came a road construction delay, then a fender bender snarled up traffic. Crawling along the roadway, she had plenty of time to think, and it still struck her as significant that the last three thefts had been within such a close geographical range. The first six had been spread out, with the only common denominators being "small" and "private" and "East Coast."

It was late afternoon by the time she arrived at the

Alliance. Owned by collectors who specialized in antique needlework, it was on the first floor of an early-nineteenth-century building on the National Register, in another pretty part of Old City that was a solid horizon of brown brick, window boxes, black ironwork, and trees.

She'd thoroughly investigated the gallery back in April—when she and Vincent had first met—but now she wanted to check for similarities that tied this building with the one that housed Champion and Stone.

Claudia walked around to the narrow brick alleyway at the back. While the row houses didn't have much in the way of landscaped grounds, window boxes overflowed with impatiens, marigolds, and petunias. The paned windows on the side facing the street, as well as the big bay window in front, were secured, but there'd been no evidence of a forced entry or exit at the time.

This afternoon, someone had propped open the back door with a broken brick, probably to let in fresh air. Not smart. From what she remembered, this door was secured against entry from the outside only and led to a public bathroom and a small office but not the sales floor itself.

The back alley had enough room next to the Dumpster for a couple of cars to park. It was mainly a service drive accessed by delivery and garbage trucks. Nothing unusual, but then, there'd been nothing unusual about Champion and Stone's back entrance setup, either—

not until she got wind of suspicious Dumpster activity.

Claudia briefly considered not warning the gallery employees about the open door. If they hadn't learned their lesson from the earlier theft, it was their problem, not hers. Nor was it her job to police every instance of idiotic behavior she encountered.

An instant later, her conscience kicked in.

With a sigh, she walked through the back door, careful to make plenty of noise just in case the lesson the gallery owners *had* learned came in the form of a shotgun.

Within seconds, a woman's voice called, "Richard? Richie, is that you?"

"No Richie back here," Claudia answered and waited as footsteps hurried her way. A small, overly tanned woman in her late sixties—Claudia recognized her as the owner-manager—poked her head into the room, surprise stamped on her face as Claudia chirped, "Hi!"

The woman's eyes widened. "Who are you? My goodness, you shouldn't be back here! This is for employees only."

"The back door's propped open with a brick. All of Philly could wander in here and help themselves to that." She motioned to the big, old-fashioned desk, where a half-empty box of donuts sat next to a sleek new laptop, both of which were surrounded by sloppy stacks of paper. "Or they could help themselves to just about anything in the place."

"Richie!" The woman's shock dissolved into annoyance. "The man doesn't have the good sense that God gave a goat, I swear! And . . . hey, wait a sec. I know you."

Claudia wasn't surprised that the woman remembered her, and not because she flattered herself that she was so unforgettable. There'd been some shouting—definitely the kind of shouting that people remembered.

"I'm Claudia Cruz, and you're Ms. Rose Dempsey, correct? I investigated a theft at your establishment back in April, on behalf of your insurance provider."

Recognition showed on Ms. Dempsey's face. "Yes! Oh, yes, I remember. How could I forget? What a horrible day." Then, recalling what had brought her into the back office to begin with, the woman added hastily, "This isn't something that happens frequently *at all*. I wouldn't tolerate it, I assure you. I'll speak to the employee in question as soon as he returns and stress how irresponsible it is to leave doors open."

"Especially in light of what happened."

"Yes." Rose looked uncomfortable at having been caught with her pants down, so to speak. Then, eyes narrowing, she went on the defensive and said, in a frosty tone, "You never got our sampler back."

"Not yet, no," Claudia admitted.

"Have you made any progress at all?"

Claudia held back a smile, aware that the woman was trying to turn attention from her own negligence by insinuating that Claudia was inept.

She could've been nasty about it, but she wasn't in the mood. Besides, she had an idea she wanted to explore: a little niggling possibility that had been darting about in her head.

"Yes." Only a little lie. More an embellishment of a burgeoning possibility than a lie, really. "Have you upgraded your security yet?"

Rose glanced away. "Somewhat. We're still working on it. Business hasn't been as brisk as we'd hoped this summer, and—"

"That's okay; just asking. As long as you get a few cameras in here, that'll help keep your insurance people happy." Claudia perched on the edge of the desk. "There's something I want to ask you, though, and it relates to the theft."

"Ask away, but we need to go back to the main gallery room. I'm a little short-staffed today and we're busy."

"No problem." Claudia waited as Rose shut the back door, then followed her to the gallery. It was small, consisting of a main room stuffed with antiques, mostly textiles. A stairway to the second floor was cordoned off. Claudia recalled there were more storage rooms up there, along with an employee lounge and a small bathroom.

A half dozen customers were browsing the narrow aisles under the watchful eye of a young woman at the cashier counter.

"Is there anything I can help you with?" Rose asked

the closest couple. When they smiled and said they were only browsing, she smiled back and retreated a short distance. Again, Claudia followed.

"What is your question, Ms. Cruz?"

"When I last talked to you, I recall you telling me you had a cleaning service that came once a week. The rest of the time, the employees were responsible for keeping the gallery tidy. Is that right?"

"Yes."

"And at the time of the theft, the cleaning crew was not due to arrive for several days?"

"Right. It was a Tuesday, and the cleaning service only comes on Fridays." Dempsey looked puzzled. "I remember the FBI agent telling me the maids weren't under suspicion."

"They're not." To the best of Claudia's knowledge, anyway. "No doubt you're aware of the recent incident at Champion and Stone."

"I heard about it on the news. I'm sure I speak for most in our line of business when I say that this is a most alarming trend."

"I'm working that case as well. Ms. Dempsey, could someone have remained in this building all night without being noticed and then found a way to slip outside the next day?"

The woman blinked. "I . . . I can't say for sure. I mean, I've never thought about it, but I suppose it's possible. The upstairs isn't used very much."

Claudia glanced up, recalling small, barred windows and how badly the stairs creaked. "If I'm remembering correctly, after your security alarms are activated for the night, they'll trigger a response only when someone enters from the outside and fails to provide the deactivation code. But if someone leaves from the inside, nothing happens."

"We've changed the alarms since then, but yes, that's how it worked at the time. Are you suggesting someone hid inside our shop and then walked out when nobody was around?"

"It's a theory, ma'am."

"Well, it's not one that makes much sense," Rose retorted. "Why take only the one sampler when they could've taken so much more?"

"A good point," Claudia admitted. Her fledgling theory had its possibilities, but also some logic problems. "Can't say for sure why they didn't take more."

"Are you still working with the FBI agent who was here that night? Agent Del . . . De—"

"DeLuca."

"Yes, that one."

"We're working together, but separately."

Rose gave her a strange look but said only "Well, by now I hope you've both learned to be a little more respectful to each other. I thought the way you shouted at each other that day was terribly unprofessional."

The heat of embarrassment crept up Claudia's

cheeks. Had it really been that bad? She'd been so focused on holding her ground while DeLuca was trying to push her out the door that she hadn't paid much attention to anyone else.

"We're working on that, too." Then, inclining her head toward the back room, she asked, "Do you mind if I look around the office again?"

Ms. Dempsey hesitated, then said, "I don't see why not, but please don't disturb anything. We're in the midst of an inventory."

"No problem. If you'd like, you can come with me. I'd understand if you wished to do so."

"I should probably." Turning to the cashier, she said, "Kelli, I'll be back in the office. Call me if you need me. And if Richie shows up, tell him I wish to speak with him immediately."

Back in the little office, Claudia reassessed the area, this time with an eye for hiding spots. It *was* a farfetched idea, and one she might not have considered if not for Digger Brody's info.

Her search didn't take long, as there were very few places anyone could hide. A supply closet and, if someone was thin and small, a sink cabinet in the public bathroom. Neither struck her as very feasible.

"I think that's all I needed to see, thanks," Claudia said. "If I have any more questions, can I give you a call?"

"Of course." The woman finally softened a bit. "I

do appreciate the fact that you're still working on this. We try to get information from the police, but they never have anything to say. I suppose if we haven't gotten our property back by now, we never will."

"Oh, I don't know . . . art theft's funny that way. Things sometimes turn up when you least expect it." Claudia headed toward the door, then stopped short. "One last question. I don't have my notes with me, so I can't remember details, but were you unusually busy that day at any point? Did anything happen that would have distracted you from seeing someone go upstairs or to the back office?"

Rose Dempsey folded her arms across her chest, frowning. "Oh, boy, it's been months . . . but yes, I do remember that we had a sudden spurt of business shortly before closing time. I was the only one working, because our cashier had gone home sick a little after lunchtime. I don't remember any disturbances, but it's possible that I might have missed someone who was sneaking around."

"Even with the squeaky stairs?"

The woman shrugged. "You get used to certain noises after a while. If I was busy with customers, I might not have noticed since the floors squeak a lot, too."

After leaving the Alliance Gallery, Claudia drove to Champion and Stone. Because of her run-in with Vincent, she suspected she wouldn't be welcome to stroll around the gallery. Luckily, details of the layout and security were still fresh in her mind, and she really only needed to poke around outside.

Unlike her FBI Man, she'd taken the time to check the neighborhood and ask questions about other trouble that night, which had led her to a police report of a knife fight in the area, then to Little Otis, and finally to Digger Brody.

Sometimes extra snooping paid off.

Brody claimed he'd spotted the black-clad woman walking away from the back alley Dumpster, and while he and his associates weren't model citizens—that night they'd been after a local drug dealer who owed them money—he had little reason to lie about a detail like this.

Champion and Stone took up the first floor of a turn-of-the-century building at the corner of a busy intersection, and Claudia followed the sidewalk around to the back, noting the fire escapes, Dumpster, and a few random parking spots marked PRIVATE.

Judging by the thick, cracked layers of paint on the window frames, they hadn't been opened in decades. No broken glass, no signs of forced entry, just like at Alliance.

Claudia glanced at the Dumpster, her theory taking on new possibilities. Despite Brody's claim that the black-clad woman wasn't a homeless person stealing from the trash, he could be mistaken. Dumpsters in this part of town had choice pickings. But being a sneaky bastard himself, Brody would recognize the difference between aimless wandering and deliberate sneaking about. The fact that she'd been carrying one box, rather than lugging around a garbage bag or whatever, had been odd enough to catch his attention, too. A Corinthian helmet could easily fit in a cardboard box.

Claudia noticed that both Alliance and Champion and Stone had public restrooms near the back service doors, and Dumpsters directly outside those doors. It wasn't uncommon to find bathrooms by back doors, which was why she hadn't considered it worth investigating before today, but it was easy to overlook something so utterly common.

Claudia eyed the back door, secured with an older-style keypad lock and a bright security light that activated at dusk. The lock had shown no sign of tampering, and the security firm reported no alarm had gone off that night.

What if the thief or thieves hadn't actually left the gallery with their stolen goods? What if they'd hidden the object in a bathroom trash can, careful to protect any fragile pieces with paper towel padding, knowing the trash would be emptied later that night? Then in the wee hours of the morning, they came back to pick up their prize from the Dumpster?

Risky, unless they'd observed routines and timing beforehand, but not out of the realm of believability.

At least not at the Alliance. The security at Champion and Stone was a lot tighter, and her theory didn't work so well under those conditions.

Claudia headed back to her car, deep in thought but with a buzz of excitement. Hot damn, she might be onto something!

Now all she needed to do was tease more information about Champion and Stone out of DeLuca, even if it meant swallowing her pride.

On the way back to her hotel, Claudia decided to take a detour to Macy's. If Vincent *did* show up tonight and if her negotiating skills failed her, she could always fall back on sex appeal, so she needed something appropriate to wear. And since it was related to her assignment, maybe she could even sneak it through on her expense report.

Chapter Nine

Ben Sheridan didn't much like being a guest of honor at fund-raisers or giving speeches. He performed his civic responsibilities often enough to stay in the public eye, but not so much that he became a gossip page regular.

Tonight's gala—in a private banquet room that looked much like any other banquet room of the tony restaurants and upscale hotels he'd visited—involved raising money for an up-and-coming young pol. Ben was local money, and because he didn't often attend these events, his appearance helped set a higher plate price. Besides, many attendees had eligible daughters or sisters, and Ben was still single after his divorce ten years ago.

Since local wealthy business folk attended the fund-raiser, he'd trotted out his standard global business market survival speech, tweaked it with newer graphs and stats, and everyone had been politely receptive. Most guests were already familiar with running companies abroad, and tonight's meeting only required a token speech. Once the speaking and political point making were out of the way, the guests toasted, the wine poured and first course served, talk and gossip and debate began to flow. His job done, Ben sat back and let the noise flow around him as he enjoyed a good meal.

The young pol seated beside him was the chatty type and maintained a constant conversation with multiple people. Ben was content to let him keep on talking. By the time dessert arrived, however, it had become apparent that the hard-eyed cougar in the off-the-shoulder blue gown, the one with the pretty blond daughter in tow, was intent on closing in on him.

His sister Ophelia was right: he should find the time to get married again. Unfortunately, his lifestyle required a woman who could keep secrets, who possessed an iron will, and who could cope with a *lot* of lonely nights.

Slim pickings here, given those criteria.

Then his cell phone vibrated. With an apologetic smile, he pulled it out. "Sheridan."

"Ben, it's Ellie. We have a situation. I need to transfer you a sensitive call."

Ah, shit, he didn't like the tone of her voice. "Okay. Give me a moment to find a quiet place and I'll call you right back."

He quickly made his apologies, and by the time he'd slipped out of the banquet room, Shaunda was waiting for him at the main entrance, the engine of the big black SUV humming behind her.

She opened the door for him and asked, "Where to, Mr. Sheridan?"

"Back to the office," he answered as he hit Redial. The second Ellie answered, he demanded, "I'm in the car and on the way back. Who wants to talk to me?"

"The first-floor receptionist transferred this one up. It's Russ Noble, one of our guides in Peru."

Ben tensed. Dead or kidnapped hikers came to mind: his main nightmare, given the nature of adventure tours. Most were relatively tame, but others were much riskier. In the fifteen years he'd been running Sheridan Expeditions, there'd been only two incidents leading to deaths, one due to faulty climbing gear and the other a small plane crash that had killed the pilot and two of four passengers.

"All right, put him through." There was a click, then another. "Russ, are you there? This is Ben Sheridan."

"Yeah, uh, Mr. Sheridan, I'm here."

The connection wasn't very good, and Ben had to strain to hear. "Is something wrong, Russ?"

"I'm afraid so . . . my partner, Stuart, is missing."

Stuart Wilcox was the other tour guide—and, like Russ Noble, he *was* only a tour guide, not an operative masquerading as a guide.

"What happened?"

"I don't know. We stayed up late last night going over plans for today, then headed to our rooms. When he didn't come down for breakfast, I figured he'd overslept or wasn't feeling well. I went to check his room, and he wasn't there. I've looked all over for him, but he's just gone. It doesn't look like his bed was even slept in."

"Have you gone to the police?"

"Yes, hours ago. They're looking into it, but so far nothing's turned up, and I have twenty-four people wondering what's going on. What do you want me to do?"

"Sit tight. I'll get a replacement down there as soon as possible, along with a lawyer to make sure everyone's taken care of." Those tourists had paid *very* well for their privately guided trip; they needed to be kept happy. "What have you told your group about the delay?"

"I told them that Stuart got sick and we took him to the hospital but that we wouldn't be delayed long and the itinerary should remain unchanged. They don't know he's missing yet, but if the police don't find him soon and this hits the local news, they will."

"All right, you're doing good so far. Keep to your story, but tell them Stuart's too sick and the company is sending a replacement; they'll be reimbursed for any losses. That should keep them from getting too restless until the new guide arrives. After that, you just get back on schedule like nothing happened."

"Yes, sir."

"Keep me informed if you hear anything else. I'll give you my secretary's direct number. Even if I'm out of the office, she'll get a message to me right away." Ben gave the guide Ellie's main number, asked for the name and number of the police official who was handling Wilcox's disappearance, and then hung up.

"Goddammit." With a sigh, Ben called Ron Levine's cell. When he answered, Ben said, "We have trouble in Peru, and I need you down there right away."

A brief silence followed. "Good thing I haven't un- packed from the last trip. What's happened?"

"One of my guides, Stuart Wilcox, has gone miss- ing."

"Local trouble?"

"Probably, but we need to get a replacement down there fast and soothe any feathers before they get ruf- fled. Do whatever's necessary to keep the hikers happy. You'll have to follow up with the police. Hopefully they've already alerted the U.S. authorities."

"Who's going to contact the missing guide's family?"

Ben briefly closed his eyes, dreading the call. "Me."

"Power has its privileges and its price," Levine said. "I take it I'll get the private jet?"

"Yes. Ellie will handle the travel details, but track- ing down a replacement guide might take a little time."

"No problem," Levine said. "It'll give me a chance to brush up on Peruvian law. Don't worry. I'll take care of your hikers, and I'll do everything I can to find Wilcox and get him back home. One way or another."

Dead or alive, in other words. "Keep me posted."

Chapter Ten

Wednesday evening, Philadelphia

Claudia walked into the lobby bar fifteen minutes late. To her annoyance, she couldn't make any kind of grand entrance because the place was packed with attendees from an art history convention. She had nothing against cutting loose and having a good time, but she wished they'd picked another weekend.

If Vincent hadn't found a table, would he have decided to stick around anyway? If he'd already left, she'd wasted her efforts to find the perfect SLBD—slinky little black dress—not to mention spent more time than she cared to admit on her hair and makeup. Why she'd gone to such trouble, she didn't know. He'd probably show up in his usual work suit, all black and white, severe and faintly rumpled.

All the things that perversely drew her to him.

Moving through the crowd of chatting conference goers, smiling politely at the compliments sent her way by tongues loosened with booze, she searched for Vincent and finally glimpsed him. Relief rushed through her, then satisfaction at the prospect of making him squirm for arresting her. Yes, she'd broken a law, but it was a stupid law when it came to people like her, and he knew it.

As Claudia threaded her way past the bodies, a hand landed too close to her ass to be accidental and a man's laughing voice said, "Honey, that's some dress!" She gritted her teeth and kept moving, resisting the urge to slug the creep. She managed to go only a few more feet before someone bumped into her from behind forcefully enough to knock her forward, and she nearly fell.

Holding on to her temper—and a string of profanity—she turned to see a woman with dark mahogany hair stumble past her, too drunk to notice what she'd done. The woman wore a red dress that played up her long legs. Helluva tall girl.

As Claudia turned away, the tall woman was joined by a petite, dark-haired woman in polka dots, who shrugged and flashed a smile as if apologizing for her companion's clumsiness. At least *someone* in this mob still had manners.

Claudia finally reached Vincent without any spilled drink adventures, additional grabby hands, or high-heeled contact sport. He didn't notice her approach and she took the opportunity to soak him in shamelessly.

It never failed to make her heart beat faster, all that lean, sleek darkness; all that tense, restless energy escaping through the long fingers turning his beer bottle in circles; and the tips of those polished black shoes tapping against the barstool footrest.

What would it take from her to release all that tension and energy until he lay languid and smiling?

Hmmm . . . her plans to make him squirm were turning more lustful than vengeful. Stupid hormones; they short-circuited her righteous ire with this man every damn time.

Claudia smoothed her dress, shook back her hair, put a smile on her face, and then squeezed between Vincent and the overweight man in a suit beside him. She couldn't avoid brushing her breasts against Vincent's arm; it was either that or her ass brushing against the hefty guy.

Vincent's eyes widened a fraction when he saw her, focusing temporarily on her cleavage before moving upward. His rueful smile tickled a heat deep inside her.

"Hey," he said in greeting.

"Hey, yourself. You're actually here. I expected you to stand me up."

"Same thought occurred to me."

"Really? This from the guy who accused me of trying to tempt him to the dark side the other night? You know, that made me feel like . . . Lex Luthor or something. Which is okay, because I liked Lex. Superman's a boring little prick, but Batman—now, I can relate to the Bat."

Uh-oh; not good . . . she was already babbling!

Vincent's smile widened to a grin. "Somehow I'm not shocked that vigilantes are more your type."

She shrugged and watched as his fascinated gaze dropped to her breasts again. Exactly the effect she wanted. She intended to maintain control in this encounter, no matter what.

"So the vigilantes weren't your type?" she asked.

"I liked Batman comics when I was a kid."

"I'm having a hard time imagining you as a kid, Vincent." A lie; she knew without a doubt he'd been a cute little brat. If nothing else, those long, curling lashes would've looked less out of place on a boy than they did on her all-grown-up FBI Man. She had fantasies about those lashes, imagined them tickling along her skin as he kissed his way down her body. "Were you this competitive and humorless even back then?"

He took a swig of his beer, brow raised. "I can't imagine you as a little girl, either. I figure you came out of the womb with stiletto heels and a sneer."

Claudia winced. "Ouch."

"Nice dress," he said, with a predatory grin and a gleam in his eyes. "What little there is of it."

"Why, thank you. Coming from you, that's almost sweet." His reaction amused her, yet it stirred surprise and unease. It was so easy to hit a verbal rhythm with this man, and she was liking it far too much. "Had a few beers while you were waiting, huh?"

"Yeah. Come to think of it, I've been spending a lot of time in bars this week."

"Is this a bad thing?"

Vincent seemed to consider the question, absently twirling his bottle. "Depends on the bar and the company."

"I'll take that as a compliment, too." She helped herself to a swig from his beer, then licked her lips, gratified when his face went slack with purely male appreciation. "By the way, Vincent, I notice you're avoiding most of my questions."

"You're also avoiding most of mine."

"True. At the rate we're going, we'll exhaust ourselves with small talk long before we get to the fun stuff."

He turned slightly to face her—and squeezed so closely together, Claudia found the full force of his dark gaze unnerving. He did not, however, rise to the bait.

Well, the night was young, and "fun" with Vincent DeLuca covered a helluva lot of territory.

"Sooo," Claudia said after a moment, drawing out the word. "Why *are* you here? You made it clear the other night that amoral trash like me aren't up to your White Knight standards."

"Going straight for blood, as always."

"It saves time," she said, then grimaced as an elbow hit her in the back. "Maybe we should take this conversation elsewhere."

"Did you have someplace in mind?"

Most certainly, probably the exact place he was thinking of, even though it might be a very bad idea. Instead, she said, "The dance floor."

"FBI agents don't dance. We just lurk and glower."

She laughed. "Okay, finish your beer, DeLuca. To preserve the dignity of the Bureau, we'll talk in my room."

"You sure you don't want something to drink? I'll buy." He tipped his head to one side. "Looks like you went to a lot of trouble to dress up for this, and unless you have somewhere else to be tonight, there's no rush."

"Is that a subtle way of asking if I have a date later?"

"No, that was my obtuse way of saying you look nice."

"Oh." Taken by surprise, she needed a moment to register his faintly expectant smile. She cleared her throat. "Thanks. To answer your question, I'll pass on the drink. There's too many people here. Someone's either gonna spill their drink down my cleavage or cop another cheap feel, and I'm not sure I'd even notice."

Vincent shifted for a better look at the big guy next to her. "I see the problem."

Going to her room was a practical alternative. It was

quiet and close by. Dinner was only a room-service call away. The room had a minibar and a table and two chairs. Even if the focal point *was* the king-size bed.

The odds were good that they'd end up in that bed. She'd been playing with the possibility on and off for four long months, and judging by the signals Vincent had sent her way, he shared her thoughts.

Did she want to go there? A rush of heat and an aching need were her answer.

As they moved through the packed bodies, Vincent's hand settled on the small of her back, and Claudia barely held off a shiver. If he could do that to her with just a polite touch, what would it be like when he was inside her?

She wore nothing beneath the dress except a black thong. Easy access for him to slip one of those long fingers under the silky band along her hip, move down along the inside of her thigh, and—

Whoa, whoa; slow down! She wanted him, and she'd have him—but she had work to do first, and indulging in fantasies wasn't helping her focus.

The reminder of work brought another problem to mind. Sleeping with the enemy was off-limits, unless it was part of an assignment, and even then Ben left the decision to the operative. While not shy about using her looks to her advantage, Claudia had never gone that far, and no way could she explain this as anything but self-indulgence.

Still, Sheridan was just the man who employed her; she had the right to hit the sheets with anyone she wanted.

Except . . . if not for Ben Sheridan, her grandparents might never have had a chance to become legal. He'd taken care of their situation simply as a courtesy toward her, changing the lives of her family overnight with casual ease. For that alone, Sheridan had her loyalty. Not to mention providing her a last chance to get it right after her career careened out of control in Dallas.

"Must be some heavy-duty thinking going on up there." Vincent's quiet voice broke through her thoughts as they crossed the lobby. "Anything that means trouble coming my way?"

"What do you know about my boss?" Claudia asked abruptly.

Surprise flashed in his eyes; then he dropped his hand from her back as he moved up beside her. "Enough to know I don't like him."

"A word of warning, Vincent. That feeling is mutual."

"Ben Sheridan doesn't scare me."

"He should. If he puts his mind to it, he can be very unpleasant. Just keep that in mind; that's all I'm saying." God, she hated being caught between her loyalty and her own desires again. "Come on. The elevator's this way."

The elevator was packed with conference goers, ending further conversation. She had no choice but to press against Vincent, close enough that she could feel him breathing, feel his heart beating. His heat surrounded her, his belt buckle pressed against the small of her back—and something else pushed against her bottom.

As Claudia glanced around the elevator, checking to see if anyone had picked up on the lust she swore must be zinging in the air, she met the gaze of a woman about her age.

"Your dress is gorgeous. I wish I had the body to wear something like that. And the nerve." The woman's eyes met Vincent's, and she smiled knowingly. "I sure hope he appreciates your efforts."

"He does."

Claudia didn't turn to look at Vincent, but she heard the amusement in his voice, and, to her amazement, heat suffused her cheeks. She hadn't blushed like this since her *quinceañero*, in her frothy white gown and twinkling tiara, dancing with *Papi* as her *mami* dabbed away proud tears. She'd felt as beautiful as any princess, finally a grown-up woman, spinning wild dreams all through the night . . .

So many years had gone by, so much had happened. She no longer recognized that girl in herself, and had stopped looking for her a long, long time ago.

The elevator lurched to a stop on every floor from the lobby to the eighth, her floor. Whenever the door opened with a soft chime, people shuffled and squeezed as a few wiggled out and others wiggled in; while she wasn't deliberately teasing Vincent by pressing against him, the end result was pretty much the same.

It was a miracle that neither of them combusted right there.

Finally, the door chimed on her floor and she snaked her way out, Vincent close behind her for obvious reasons. Imagining what might be going through his mind right now made it difficult not to smile. Tonight's dress had served its purpose well.

He stepped aside as she ran the card through her door slot, and then they were inside in the cool darkness. Claudia felt around for the light switch, filling the room with a pale glow.

"Much better! Philadelphia in the summer, the city of conventions. I should've arranged to meet you elsewhere."

Vincent, hands in his pockets, followed her farther inside. "Doesn't matter to me. I'm used to crowds."

"Really?" Claudia debated where to sit and finally leaned against the bureau. With the mirror behind her, he could have an unobstructed view of front and back. It also kept him in plain sight, exactly where she wanted him. "I would've pegged you for the crowd-avoidance type."

"I get along great with people. I even give talks and seminars at conventions, universities, and museums.

We Art Squad guys make nice with the general public. Unlike your people."

Ah, yes. Back to that. "Vincent, before we go any further, you really need to answer my question. When I asked to work with you, you turned me down flat. The reason you gave basically comes down to I'm working for the spawn of Satan. So what's with the big change of heart, and why should I believe you aren't just making nice so you can screw me over?"

Perhaps not the best choice of words. An awkward moment passed before she added, "By that, I mean take my work and use it for yourself. The other kind of screwing isn't likely to piss me off. Not if you do it right, anyway."

He opened his mouth, shut it, then scrubbed a hand over his face. "I'm no stranger to blunt women, but you take the prize. And you're right. I owe you an answer."

"Yeah, and an apology wouldn't be such a bad idea, either."

Loudly blowing out a breath, Vincent said, "I'm not going to apologize for my belief in basic ethics, or for trying to hold on to it as best I can in a world that doesn't seem to care much about anything."

"I'm not asking you to do that. I never would. All I want is for you to add a little more gray to that black-and-white view of yours."

He leaned against the wall opposite her. "Fair enough. And, in the spirit of fairness, I apologize for acting as if what I did was for any other reason than to prove a point."

"Which would be that you're the one with the genuine, USA-government-approved power and authority." When he shrugged, still obviously uncomfortable, Claudia sighed. "I know what I am, Vincent, and I have no illusions that what I do doesn't skirt the edge of legalities and ethics."

"And what you do is something I can't support. No, wait. Let me finish." He raised his hand. "I'm still working through this in my head, but I admit I haven't been straight with you. Maybe I can't fully support your methods, but I'm trying to accept that your way of working is part of a reality, even if it's a reality I don't want to see."

The honesty stirred her sympathy, and what little anger still lingered, faded. "Avalon wouldn't exist if there wasn't a need for it. There's been a need for it for a very long time."

"I know."

His strained tone hinted at what it had cost him to admit even that much.

"I wish it were easier to make the world a safer place for people, not to mention for art and old things that sometimes don't seem so important when stacked up against all the other evil shit that goes down around us every day," she said softly. "In the end, though, we can only do what we can and hope it's enough. Yeah, I can move more freely than you, but all you gotta do is flash your FBI cred and a lot of important doors open wide for you."

She took a quick breath, then added, "To be honest, there are days I get real tired of having to beat down those doors over and over again. So in a way, I guess I'm a little jealous of you."

Vincent smiled. "I was thinking along those lines myself not so long ago."

It took a moment before his meaning sank in. "Really? You're jealous of *me?*"

"More like envious." He hesitated. "There are days when I think I'd like to know what it's like not to have to follow the rules. To solve problems more . . . directly."

"Winging it isn't all it's cracked up to be," Claudia said after a moment, amazed all over again. "And a lot of the time, I'm caught up in the same routine shit that you deal with."

"Thanks, but that's not true. I don't run around Philly in the dead of night with a suppressor." He frowned. "And what the hell were you doing, anyway?"

Claudia smiled. "If I answer, it means we're working together, right?"

"Yes. If you want to work with me, I'll play as fair as I can and expect the same from you. No more, no less. Deal?"

Panic rose briefly as she wondered if she even remembered what it was like to play fair.

"Deal." It still felt like *High Noon*, with her on one side of the corral and him on the other. He was all business, and she let out a short sigh. "I owe you an apology, too. I've been doing my best to get under your skin, and sometimes I get a little carried away with the sex-fu stuff."

Confusion flashed across his face. "What?"

"You know, like kung fu, only with sex. Seduction and sex as a weapon." Again, her face warmed. "It's kind of a joke."

"Ah." His gaze took in her dress. Slowly. "This sex fu of yours has great power."

"And yet you resist! Your self-control has great power as well, O mighty FBI Man."

Vincent laughed, breaking the tension. A small thing, coaxing out that laugh, and Claudia was absurdly pleased to have succeeded.

"Okay," she said. "Now that we've both acknowledged the elephant in the room, let's get back to safe, work-related subjects."

She moved to the table, motioning him to join her. "To answer your question, I was talking with a low-level mob fence named Digger Brody. He doesn't live in a nice part of town, and he's not such a nice guy, so I had to be prepared to show him I meant business."

"The name sounds familiar." Vincent sat, pushing back from the table to stretch out his legs.

Claudia tried not to notice how the material of his

suit failed to disguise those long, lean muscles, or to allow that loosened tie—and peek of skin at the hollow of his throat—to distract her. What was wrong with her, that a mere dip between the collarbones left her hot and bothered?

She cleared her throat. "It should be familiar, since he fences stolen jewelry and collectibles to his connections in Jersey and Miami. He also dabbles in drug dealing and extortion, which was what he was doing the night the helmet went missing at Champion and Stone. He was with two men that night; there was a fight, and one of them tried to claim that the drugs really belonged to a woman they saw sneaking out of an alley behind the gallery."

Vincent was staring at her. "How'd you hear about this?"

"I asked around to see if anything else happened that night. Mostly, I just got lucky." When he continued to stare, she added defensively, "What? Dumb luck happens sometimes, you know? I'm good at my job, but I'll take whatever I can get. Anyway, I heard about the fight, persuaded the responding officer to answer a few questions, then started poking around and flashing money until I turned up a couple of names. One name led to another, and then me and Brody had a talk at his apartment."

"A woman," Vincent said, eyes narrowing. "There was a woman in the alley."

"Yup. Brody said she came out from behind the Dumpster by the gallery, dressed in dark clothes and carrying a box. He was insistent she wasn't a homeless woman digging around in the trash. He wasn't real forthcoming with the details, but it's a start."

"And that's all you've got?"

The question stung—and it didn't help any that he sounded extra smug. "No," she retorted. "I also took another look around the Alliance and Champion and Stone galleries today. I know it doesn't sound very important, but both buildings have Dumpsters right outside and restrooms located right by the back doors. The stolen items could've been hidden in the bathroom trash inside the galleries. After the trash was emptied into the Dumpsters, it would be easy enough to retrieve it very early in the morning, when there's less traffic and before the garbage trucks came by."

"That would be one way to explain why there's been no evidence of forced entry," Vincent said, after a moment.

"Exactly. I'm thinking the thieves are working during regular hours. I don't know exactly how, but it's my best guess." Warming up to her theory, Claudia leaned forward. "I was also wondering about the location trending. The thefts have been random and geographically spread out except for these last three. I wonder if they've started targeting the Philly area on purpose."

"And why would that be?"

"Because of the challenge of having FBI Art Squad agents in the city? It wouldn't be the first time the bad guys taunted the good guys."

The expression on his face told her he was considering the possibility, and seeing it gave her a kind of crazy buzz. She knew her theories were solid and to see him acknowledge it pleased her no end. Until now, she hadn't realized how bad she'd wanted him to see her as an equal, to have his respect.

"Okay, DeLuca. Your turn."

Vincent folded his arms over his chest, the seams of his suit jacket pulling tight across his shoulders. "I found something on the security data yesterday, and it happens to reinforce your theory."

Vindication! How sweet it tasted. "Looks like we're off to a good start with this partner thing."

"Uh-huh . . . and, like you, I suspect the thieves are making their moves during regular working hours. When I was examining the Champion and Stone data again, I noticed a man in a gray suit walk into the gallery, but none of the cameras recorded him leaving."

"Could it be a blind spot? It looked to me like most, if not all, of the thefts were located in camera blind spots, either completely or partially."

He stared at her for a moment. "No, I checked that. There are only two entrances to the gallery, and both are under full surveillance. Gray Suit never left. And this is where things get potentially interesting." He sat forward as well, elbows on the table, his clasped hands only inches from her own. "As I went over footage from the next day, when Arnetta discovered the helmet had been stolen, I spotted a woman leaving the gallery, but none of the cameras had recorded her coming inside."

"Well, well," Claudia said, arching a brow. "Looks like we got us a tag team."

"From what you just told me, I agree it's likely a team—and at least one of them can pass for another gender well enough to throw off investigators and confuse witnesses."

"Remaining inside and leaving again during regular hours would explain how they're bypassing the tougher security. Was the gallery manager distracted during both of these instances on the tapes?"

He nodded. "Whoever they are, and however many there are, they're well-organized. Each hit was carefully planned."

"Huh." She tapped her nails on the table, thinking. "At Alliance, someone could've easily left the stolen sampler in the public bathroom. The employees do light cleaning on the days when there's no janitor service, and they would've thrown the garbage bag into the Dumpster. Not sure how it would work at Champion and Stone, but if this is how these incidents are going down, then we have a methodology to work with."

"You're right." He gave her a slow grin. "Good work."

Claudia grinned back. "It sounds like a professional

outfit, except they're only stealing from wherever the security is weakest. Does that say professional to you, or does it say impulse and a quick buck?"

"It says they don't care what they steal, as long as they can eventually sell it, but they're planning ahead. It's says pragmatic to me. Even if they started out on a quick-buck impulse, they've refined their efforts."

"Getting greedy and cocky. I love it when that happens, because that's when they start making mistakes. Brody swears it's not local business and says he hasn't seen any of the stolen property. I tend to believe him. He set up a meeting with me this afternoon to pass on more info about our Lady in Black, but he didn't show."

"They could have their own means of moving the property, waiting until the investigation cools down before they try to sell it off," Vincent said. "It's standard operating procedure for these types of thefts."

It was nice to be talking shop with someone, nice not to be alone, even if only for a brief period. "Now I *really* want to see those security recordings. I don't suppose there's any chance you can be persuaded to—"

"I can bring home backup copies of the few that I have. I'd appreciate any help you can offer, because the Bureau doesn't have a lot of agents to spare at the moment."

"Now that we have an idea of what to look for, we'll find something. I've got a good feeling about this." She grinned at him, and almost laughed when he grinned back. "This calls for a celebration."

"Because we're finally on the right track?"

"Yes, and also because we managed to talk for five minutes straight without insulting or arresting each other. I don't know about you, but a few days ago, I'd have put the chance of that happening at zero." Claudia kicked off her heels with a sigh of relief, then headed toward the minibar. "Let's see what we have . . . There must be a bottle or two of champagne in here."

Vincent followed, standing so close that she could feel his heat. Straightening with two mini bottles in each hand, she turned to face him. Even when she was prepared for it, his nearness took her breath away.

He was right: it was time to play fair. No more games, no more trying to outmaneuver him. So when the silence lengthened, she simply said what needed saying: "Or did you have another kind of celebration in mind?"

Chapter Eleven

Vincent felt certain her thoughts were moving along the same lines as his, but with this woman it was smarter to make sure. "To be honest, yeah. But I'm not sure what you have in mind."

"Oh, Vincent. Please." Claudia laughed softly. "From the first time we met, I've been wondering what it would be like to get you in my bed. You know that."

Her bluntness knocked him off-balance. But the craziness and unpredictability was part of the attraction; a relationship of any sort with Claudia would never be dull.

"It would've been ungentlemanly to assume."

"Ungentlemanly?" She stared at him. "Now *there's* a word I don't hear very often, especially from any man under seventy."

He meant it, even if her expression broadcast her doubts. Not that he could blame her, since his fantasies had been mostly of the wham-bam-adios-ma'am variety. So why the insane self-restraint now?

Because at some point he'd crossed the line from resenting the hell out of her to wanting her in his life—dammit, this was going to lead to nothing but trouble.

Knowing it didn't stop him from taking the little bottles out of her hands. As he put them aside, he leaned closer, picking up on the tension humming off her. "What do you want, Claudia?" When her brows arched, he added with a laugh, "Besides sex. We're clear on that part."

She looked puzzled, then her eyes softened before she glanced away. "Mostly I want to get you out of that suit, one button at a time. I've had my share of lovers, Vincent. I know what I want and why. The game and the chase has been half the fun, but what I want . . ."

Vincent waited, noting how she'd eased back and wouldn't meet his eyes. She was still so close, though, and all he had to do was take her hips in his hands and pull her against him. She wouldn't resist. The temptation to do so seized him on a hot, heady rush of desire, but he didn't move. For some reason, it was important that she come to him.

What *did* she want? More action, less talk? More romance, fewer complications?

"I want to be smart about this," she finally said. "We have this conflict of interest, and as much as I tell myself to ignore it, it's always there, nagging at me. It shouldn't be an issue. If we sleep together, who's gonna care except me and you? I know it's better to just carpe diem and all that shit, but I still want—"

Again she broke off, looking frustrated and embarrassed.

"C'mon, Claudia. Something's bothering you. Tell me," he urged.

"I guess I want *more*. For the first time in a really, really long time, Vincent, I want more than just grabbin' at a flash of opportunity or living in the moment." She huffed, tipping her head back and closing her eyes. "So naturally, the one man who makes me want all this is the one who won't fit neatly into my life! I should stick to Avalon men. At least they'd know not to expect too much from me."

The "one man" part pleased him with a visceral male possessiveness he'd never experienced before. "So why don't you hook up with guys like the lawyer?"

A quick half smile. "Because most of Sheridan's boys are crazy. I know we all have to be a little crazy to do what we do, but they're not my type, as in 'we'd kill each other within five minutes' not my type. The ones that are my type are already taken."

"I got the impression you'd filed me under not your type."

"Maybe at first, but the urge to get you naked overrode the urge to do you bodily harm." She put a small distance between them. "Vincent, what's with all the questions? I was more or less expecting you to just shove me onto the bed and have at it."

"So was I," he admitted.

She blinked, then laughed. "Instead, we're both acting like a couple of shy kids on a first date." Motioning toward the little champagne bottles, she added, "You could always get me drunk."

"These won't get you drunk enough to blame the booze for any regrets you might have later." Vincent took her hand, and slid it down the front of his pants so she could feel his erection. "For the record, I'm not shy and I don't need a drink to loosen my inhibitions."

Claudia stroked him lightly, making him suck in his breath. Christ, if she could affect him like this with only a touch, what would it be like to feel her mouth around him? To bury himself deep inside her?

"I never thought you had any inhibitions, DeLuca. Control issues, hell yeah—but no inhibitions."

"Control issues?"

Amusement glinted in her eyes. "Like you don't know that."

"That's a good thing for you, then, since you're sending me mixed signals and it's taking all my control not to put my hands where I want to."

"One of my fantasies is to make you give up all that control to me. I'd tie your hands with that skinny black tie of yours and make you close your eyes. Or better yet, I'd tie back your hands with that belt and blindfold you with the tie." She pressed against him, all heat and curves and invasive perfume, clouding his head with every sensation but the taste of her. "Then I'd make you beg."

Equal parts lust and denial, hot and cold, washed over him. "I've never begged for anything in my life."

"Really?" Her gaze locked on his as she squeezed him hard through his pants. As he hissed out a breath, she added, "But maybe you want to."

Did he? He'd enjoyed playful sex before, along with rougher sex when the mood took him or his partner asked for it. Toys were a turn-on, and he was always game for watching a lover play with herself, but this suggestion made him uneasy. "Interesting proposition, but I don't think I'd like my hands tied."

"See?" She looked smug. "Control issues."

"No," he retorted, strangely defensive. What the hell? It wasn't as if he needed to apologize for not being into kink. "That kind of sex . . . it's not me."

"It's not my bliss, either, but I like to play, be a little bad."

"I could always tie *you* up," he murmured.

"Uh-uh, it doesn't work that way," she whispered with a sly smile. "See, I have no control issues."

Vincent laughed; he couldn't help it. "The hell you don't."

Then, to mess with her expectations, he leaned down and brushed his mouth along her chin, her lips, and then took her mouth in a deep, leisurely kiss.

For so long, he'd imagined what it would be like to

kiss her, but those thoughts were no match to the reality.

Her mouth opened invitingly, and her tongue played with his, teasing and stroking. She filled his hands, and every place where his body met hers prickled into hyperawareness. Warm, supple skin and lean muscles, firm breasts and a lush curve of hip and bottom. The smell of her perfume, the brush of her hair along his face, his beard stubble catching strands as he kissed his way to the most sensitive spot right below her ear.

She made a delicious sound deep in her throat, making him harder, and when she rocked her hips against him, he pulled up the hem of her dress until he had what he wanted: firm, warm woman skin. He ran his palms along her round bottom, cupping and kneading, finding the skinny lace band of her thong, no real barrier to exploring further, deeper.

Within moments, he'd determined she wore no bra. All he had to do was slip a strap off her shoulder and he would finally know, after months of fleeting daydreams, the taste and feel of her breasts.

As if following his thoughts, Claudia's fingernails sank into his shoulder muscles, the sharpness registering even through his shirt and suit coat, and then she had his coat off and began working on his tie.

Remembering what she'd said about his tie, he grabbed her wrists, forced her around, and then used his greater weight and height to back her into the wall. Her eyes widened as she bumped against it—harder than he'd intended—but the laugh that followed held an undeniable note of triumph.

Heat and need dampened her skin as well as his own; the cotton of his shirt was clinging, constraining. He wanted it gone, but once his shirt was off and her dress was down to her waist, there'd be no stopping this.

"You have condoms?" Claudia asked when he gave her a moment to breathe. "Because if you don't, I—"

"I'm good," he said, roughly.

"Oh, I'm sure you will be," she responded, as close to a purr as any human could go.

Desire and need narrowed everything down to the feel of her skin against his, her heat, her scent. He had her dress off in seconds, leaving her pinned to the wall in only a thong and thigh-high stockings, looking like every man's late-night fantasy.

Only this was all real: her excited breathing, the pain of her long nails as she roughly undid his shirt buttons. He shrugged clear of his shirt, then shifted his grip and hoisted her higher, bringing her breasts close.

Full and round, with large, dark nipples pinched in tight tips, just begging for his attention.

"Do it," she urged, arching her back. "C'mon!"

"Who's begging now?" He took a nipple between his teeth, rolling and tugging as she gasped and arched. Her nails closed over his shoulders hard enough to leave marks, but he barely noticed, flicking his tongue along the sensitive, aroused peaks, then sucking and nipping until she started banging her head against the wall.

He hoped no one was home next door, because they were about to make a lot of noise.

Vincent let her slide downward, taking her mouth again, and she went to work on his pants. The belt hit the carpet with a thump, then the zipper was down and she slipped her hand inside his boxers.

He squeezed his eyes so tight he practically saw stars, swearing against her wet lips as she lightly scored her nails up along his erection. He ached to get inside her, hardly able to think of anything else, but remained just aware enough to know it was time to slow down and give her more attention.

"Back pocket," he said, slipping a finger beneath the thong and following the moist trail to her hottest spot. "Get it."

It took a little maneuvering, and her surprisingly girlish giggle turned to a low hum of pleasure as his finger slid deeper within her, but she managed to snag his wallet and helped him with the condom, all without tipping them both over.

"Hold on to my shoulders," he ordered, hooking a hand around her hips for a firmer grip.

She grabbed and held on as he worked his fingers in and out of her, slowly at first, then fast and deep, his thumb sliding along her clit until he could hear her breathing increase and feel the trembles of approaching orgasm in the muscles of her arms and legs.

She came hard with a high, sharp gasp, and he didn't let up, even when she started squirming, coaxing her to another orgasm fast on the first, until she was panting and straining.

Then he turned his attention back to her breasts, gently biting and sucking as he continued to caress her, easing her to the heights of need again. He took his time, despite his own overwhelming urge to pound into her, until he sensed she was close again.

"Vincent . . . *in* me . . . I want you in me now!"

Perfect timing. He stripped off her thong, pushed her back against the wall, spreading her wider, and she grabbed him and helped him find his way inside.

Again his eyes closed and he sucked in his breath, concentrating on the tight feel of her surrounding him, savoring the slick heat. Then he began moving. Shallow, teasing thrusts for as long as he could stand it, her rapid breathing urging him to a faster pace. Her hips met his eagerly, and no matter how much he wanted this to last and last, he could already feel the tension tightening to a knot, straining for release.

Her moaning grew louder, gasping at each thrust. "Harder . . . all the way, all the way!"

He barely heard her as he thrust harder and faster, her heels knocking against the wall in a matching frenzy, and then he knew nothing but the spurting release, muscles tight with the effort, jerking against her, all of him centered in one powerful sensation for one short moment as he came. She was still working toward it, and he continued grinding against her, panting with the effort, until she finally followed with a strangled, between-clenched-teeth "Fuck, yes . . . yes!"

Then it was over. In the silence that followed, their breathing sounded unnaturally loud. He heard the blare of a TV close by, the volume turned way up. Claudia noticed at the same moment, and her eyes widened as she bit her lower lip.

"I sure hope there were no kids next door."

Still inside her, Vincent laughed softly. "A little late to worry about that. We're lucky no one banged on the door and told us to shut up."

"I was trying to be quiet."

"That was quiet?" He kissed her and then, as she settled closer against him, rested his forehead on hers. "I can't wait to get you someplace more private and hear you let go."

"I think I bruised my heels. Maybe my head, too."

"The bed, then," he said, easing her down to the floor. He stepped back, admiring her, feeling himself hardening again. "God, you're beautiful."

"So every man has said, since the dawn of time, to every woman he manages to get naked."

"I mean it."

"I know." Her gaze roamed over his own body, lingering on his dick, and she smiled slowly as it began to arch toward her. "And I know what you want."

"Can't hide it," he said, then grabbed her hand and pulled her toward the bed. He yanked down the coverlet and top sheet, then fell backward onto the mattress, pulling her down with him.

Being on top clearly met with her approval, and she took him firmly in her hand, guiding him inside her once again. He grabbed her hips, helping set the rhythm, mesmerized by the bounce of her breasts as she worked him, sometimes driving up and down, other times circling her hips, rising and falling.

With the first pounding, impatient rush of need taken care of, he could stretch out the pleasure this time. Claudia was clearly thinking along the same lines, teasing him with her movements, but she blew his control when she touched herself, one long, red fingernail stroking her clitoris as she squeezed her nipple with her other hand, tongue tracing her lips, watching him.

He shuddered, trying to hold on, but the orgasm hit with blinding speed as he yanked her hips down, his own pumping to meet her grinding, and then it spun him down and down, one trembling release after another, lasting longer than any he'd ever known before. It left him gasping and sweating, staring at her in amazement.

"Jesus," he finally managed to say. "Jesus."

"Mmmm, it was *so*, so good." Claudia flopped down beside him, rubbing her hand along his sweat-slick chest. "Nothing better than a man who cares enough to give a girl multiple orgasms. If I had any brains, I'd fall in love with you on the spot."

"Yeah," he muttered. "I'm beginning to understand why some men are so hot to get married. A guy finds someone like you, he's not going to want to give it up. Exclusive rights sound real good."

"I think that might be a bit sexist, DeLuca."

"I don't think sex this good cares about being politically correct. It just wants more, as often as possible."

She checked him out. "Not yet, looks like."

"Give me a minute. My heart's still trying to remember how to beat right."

"I think we're gonna need another rubber."

"A lot, if I get lucky."

Vincent hooked his arm around her and pulled her against him, pleasantly surprised when she snuggled tight. He hadn't pegged her as the snuggling sort. He didn't think she'd be the kind to immediately roll out of bed and run for the bathroom, but . . . Ah, hell, he never knew what to expect with Claudia.

They lay in comfortable silence for a while until Vincent rolled up onto his elbow to look down at her.

She really was beautiful. Not the waiflike, blond kind of beauty of Hollywood and fashion magazines. She was tall, lithe and muscled; he could see the tendons, the tone, beneath the smooth brown skin. Her hips were womanly, her breasts natural and on the smallish side when not pushed up to aggressive heights by an underwire bra. She had faint wrinkles at the corners of her eyes, a few scars, a mouth made for kissing and smiling, big, dark eyes a man could lose himself in, and her hair was completely, totally messed and he'd had a hand in that.

"It's okay to touch," Claudia said, her amused voice breaking his smug thoughts. "I don't mind the looking, but touching is much nicer."

"I was thinking where to begin," Vincent said, returning her lazy smile.

"Mmmm, do you need any help in deciding?"

"No," he said, leaning down to take a nipple in his mouth again, pleased at her little sigh of contentment. "Eventually"—he moved to the other breast—"I'll get to all of you. Not in any hurry. Are you?"

"Not yet," she murmured, arching slightly as she closed her eyes. "But keep that up, and I might be."

There was nothing sexier than a sexually self-confident woman. Forget all the revealing clothes and high heels and glossy lipstick that invited and promised; all he wanted was a woman who knew what *she* wanted and wasn't afraid to ask for it—and who gave as good as she got.

"Let's get you comfortable," he said, plumping pillows under her shoulders and hips. The only light in the room was the dim entry light by the door, enough for him to note the bikini wax and glimpse a gleam of moistness as he positioned her hips where he wanted them. He wanted to see all of her, every detail—but the hints, the shadows and mysterious valleys, teased in a way that was so much more satisfying.

"What are you doing?" She sounded both amused and bemused.

"Anticipation," Vincent replied, grinning. He kissed the inside of her thigh, moving upward, breathing in deeply as he moved to the other thigh and kissed his way down to her ankle.

She sighed, raising her hips in an invitation, conscious or otherwise, but he had no intention of accepting it just yet. She had pretty knees and smooth skin. So easy to slide his palms up and down her thighs, inside and out, on a friction of warmth. He imagined those strong thighs closing tight around his head as he ate her out, trapping him in a bounty of female flesh. She wanted to feel his mouth and tongue on her; he could tell by the increasing movements of her hips, straining toward him, the change in her breathing.

Mindful of the TV admonishment, she was being quiet, and watching her bite down on her lip aroused him even more. He started at her ankle and slowly kissed his way up her inner leg and thigh, satisfied to feel the slight trembling in her muscles, knowing she was thinking that *this* time he'd slide his tongue over her, hard and sure, his hot, flexible mouth on the overly sensitized flesh aching for that touch.

Instead he blew a soft breath over her, making her

squeak—a cute sound he could get to like—and then slid upward to kiss her mouth, letting his cock brush against her folds.

"You bastard," she said, punching him in the shoulder. "Do that again and I'll kill you."

Laughing, Vincent planted rapid, hard kisses down her neck and chest, teasing her nipples until she began to squirm. Then he finally moved down between her legs to give her what she wanted.

A flick of the tongue for openers, and she bucked with a moan, teeth worrying her lip again as she grabbed at the sheets, pulling them into a tight grip.

She liked that—good. He repeated it several more times, keeping his hands on her thighs, pushing them wide. Her hips rose to meet his mouth, and he licked upward slowly with increasing pressure, again and again, until she began making incoherent sounds and it was time to get serious. He tongued all of her, licking and sucking, teasing her clitoris with the tip of his tongue, then probing deeper within, taking in the taste and feel of her, her frantic motions and mewling nearly enough to make him come right then.

Claudia was taking her time to climax, trying to control the moment, to make it last. When he saw that, Vincent's mouth and tongue moved with more force and speed, as determined to make her come as she was determined to hold out. It was a contest of wills she couldn't win, and within seconds the orgasm rushed through her, her muscles trembling. He didn't let up, keeping at it, coaxing her higher, even as she pushed at his shoulders and tried to close her legs. She didn't want him to stop, her arching hips said, but caught between pleasure and oversensitization, she instinctually tried to urge him on as well as slow him down.

Her body, beautifully responsive and taut, shuddered again. Sensing how close she was to another orgasm, Vincent waited a moment longer before shifting upward and burying himself inside her. Thrusting hard and fast, he matched her rising need, watching her face, and as her mouth fell slack and she closed her eyes, lost in the pleasure, he began to climax as well.

He took her face in his hands, forcing her to look at him, to watch him lose himself in her. A split second before he came, she gave a deep, throaty laugh and whispered, "Control issues."

It took a moment before he could respond, chest heaving, still holding her face, though his thumb caressed the curve of her lips. "Maybe. But I won that round."

She grinned. "The night's still young. I'll make you beg yet."

Chapter Twelve

Thursday morning, Philadelphia

The persistent ring tone of her cell phone woke Claudia, and she sat up, groping for it as Vincent groaned and rolled over, blocking his eyes from the sudden light when she switched on the table lamp.

The alarm clock's cheery green glow proclaimed the time 6:05 AM. Hideously early. "Cruz. What?"

"Did I wake you up?"

The drily amused voice on the other end belonged to Ben. Jesus, it was only three in the morning in Seattle! The man had to be a cyborg.

"Yeah, you did, but it's okay." She glanced at Vincent's broad back and tousled hair, doubting he was as sound asleep as he looked. She held back a sigh. "If you got something important for me, though, I'm not alone. Maybe I should call you back."

She held her breath, worried Ben would guess who she was with, and braced herself for his reaction. Instead, after an uncomfortably long pause, he said, "Nothing important. Just a heads-up that I've got details on that new job in Texas. I need you out there today. Whatever you're working on in Philly will have to wait."

A sinking feeling washed over her. She'd known this was coming but had expected a little advance warning. "Can you give me a couple more days? A new lead's come up here and it's looking good. I don't want to lose the momentum."

"It's not something the locals can handle? Like that asshole Fed of yours? What's his name again . . . DeLuca?"

"No, it's not, and no, he can't," Claudia said without hesitation, even as she cringed inwardly at the blatant lie.

Another heavy, pregnant pause, the kind that told her he knew she was lying. Claudia waited again for the anger and recriminations—and, again, they didn't happen.

"One day. No more than that. You can always get back to Philly later." Ben's tone was terse, brooking no further argument. "Ellie will send the assignment details by courier. You should have that by this afternoon. Our liaison was expecting to see you tonight, but I can stall for a day."

"Thanks. I appreciate it."

"If the delay means catching the thieves, that'll be thanks enough. Keep me posted on what's going on." He disconnected.

Claudia dropped her hand to the sheets, slowly letting out her breath. After a moment, she asked quietly, "You awake?"

"I am now." Vincent rolled over, stretching, and it had the effect on her that he no doubt intended. If not for the fact that they both had work to do, she'd have pulled the sheet away and followed his happy trail down to a little morning delight. The sonofabitch deserved it, after all that delicious teasing last night. "I take it you're leaving soon?" he asked.

"Something's going down in Texas." How much to tell him? They were on the same side, in all the ways that counted, but she knew Ben would feel otherwise. "No real details yet."

In the dim light, she couldn't read Vincent's shadowed face. He sat up, arms resting across his sheet-draped knees. "If I'm remembering right, there's been a string of thefts from churches down that way. Somebody stealing relics."

"That's low."

He shrugged. "The world's full of low-life bastards."

"Believe me, I know all about it." She pushed her hair back, hoping she didn't look too awful. The real test of any relationship was the reality of the morning after. She could tell he was trying not to stare at her bare breasts, and she couldn't decide if that was a good thing . . . or not.

The silence turned awkward, and Vincent glanced

at the clock. "I should get going. I'll head to the office first to pick up copies of the security data, then how about I meet you at my place at around seven-thirty?"

So much for postcoital coos and sweet nothings. It was to be expected; they'd both had an itch in need of scratching, and now that it had been soothed, it was time to float back down to the ho-hum of the everyday routine.

She'd thought the sex had been great, but maybe he'd had better. Strangely self-conscious of her nudity, she turned away. "I need a shower. Worked up a hell of a sweat last night. If I didn't mention it before, thanks for the good time. It was very nice."

As she pushed up off the mattress, a big, warm hand settled on her belly and pulled her back down.

"Hey," he said, softly, as he settled her against his chest. "You okay?"

I am now that you're holding me, the foolishly infatuated part of her whispered inside her head. "Yeah. Why wouldn't I be?" she asked, eyebrow raised as she glanced over her shoulder at him. "You worked hard to make sure of that."

Despite her affected nonchalance, she couldn't help closing her eyes briefly when he rolled a nipple between his fingers. From self-doubt to lust in five seconds flat—not a good sign. This man was going to be no end of trouble. She'd always known that but had grossly underestimated the sum total.

"Just checking." He kissed her shoulder, a soft brush of lips. "I'm not sure what to do here. I've never slept with the enemy before."

"I'm not your enemy, Vincent."

"No," he said, after a moment. "But I'm not sure you're a hundred percent on my side, either."

"Goes both ways, homeboy."

Whatever ambivalence he felt toward her work, it didn't extend to her body. He teased her nipple again, filling her instantly with a hot, liquid need. "If you want," he said, his breath warm on her neck, "I can check into what we have on the church thefts down in Texas if that's what it turns out to be."

Her surprise quickly turned to unease. "You can't do that; you'll get in trouble. I can handle my assignments without the FBI's help. I've been doing so for years." Realizing how cold that sounded, she added quickly, "But I appreciate the thought. I really do."

"I wasn't offering you any actual files," he said. "I know better than that. All I meant was that we might be able to help each other out from time to time, and if we're careful, it won't earn me another reprimand and you won't piss off your psycho boss."

It was hard to think when he kept touching her like this.

"Ben's not psycho," Claudia said automatically. Then, frowning, she turned. "What reprimand?"

"I keep getting warned to stop harassing you."

"Really?"

"Really. Which is ironic, considering you're always the one coming after *me*." His smile didn't quite reach his eyes. "Last time, my supervisor told me to sleep with you if that's what it took to get you out of my system."

"Did he now." Claudia didn't miss the watchful intensity of Vincent's expression. "That's very . . . interesting."

"I thought so."

"Except that while *your* boss might be encouraging a working liaison, mine would be more inclined to get your ass reassigned to a place where you'd never see me again."

Vincent went still. "He'd do that?"

"Maybe, maybe not. But I guarantee he could disrupt your life in a lot of little ways that would add up to one major annoyance. I told you not to underestimate him; if you stand in his way, he'll go through you rather than around you. I've seen him do it."

Vincent swore softly, clearly angry.

"I can probably persuade him to back off. He's not unreasonable," Claudia said, feeling strangely defensive of Ben, even if he didn't need it—or would want her defending him. "But he's one very determined man, and people like that . . . you handle them carefully. It's just the smart thing to do."

"The FBI would like to get some hold over him."

"I bet they would. I'm sure your boss hopes I'm a potential weak link, and that's why he's telling you to be a little nicer to me."

"I don't think my boss considers you weak in any sense of the word, Claudia."

"When it comes to sex, all bets are off. There's a long, sad history of sex bringing down the smartest women and the strongest men."

"So how come your boss isn't encouraging you to sleep with me and use your sex-fu wiles to tease information out of me?"

His tone was light but not entirely convincing. All those warm, lustful feelings of a moment ago had faded. It was hard for a girl to get into the moment if a little careless pillow talk could bring down the empire of the man who had saved her ass more than once.

"Ben won't care if I want a fling with you, but I can't say he'd feel the same way about anything more serious." Which was a stupid thing to say; when had either of them expected this would be anything but a brief, if intense, affair?

Too late now to take the words back, though. Claudia sighed. "And, as much as I hate to admit it, he wouldn't be above using the situation to his advantage if an opportunity presented itself. I admire Ben Sheridan, and I am two hundred percent loyal to the man, but I don't always trust his intentions."

Vincent grunted. "You're smarter than me. I trusted my boss to play it straight with me."

Saddened to see the tarnish of cynicism taking its toll, she leaned over and kissed him. "It's not about smarts, Vincent. Your problem is that you believe your peers share your code of honor. You trust too easily, but that's not anything to be ashamed of. You should be proud of it, and it's too bad people like you are the exception rather than the norm."

"Thanks for the vote of confidence." He paused. "And on what side do you fall in all this?"

Another honest, sincere question that deserved an answer in kind. Carefully choosing her words, she said, "I'm as honest as I need to be at any given time. If you put your trust in me, I will do everything in my power not to betray that trust. I'd hurt myself before I hurt any innocents—I can promise you that. In my own way, I try to be good enough."

After a moment, he nodded. "That's about all any of us can do—try to be good enough." He glanced at her. "Which reminds me of something I've been meaning to ask you about."

The tone of voice was warning enough, and she knew what was coming. "The Dallas thing," she said flatly.

"Yeah. I would really like to know the truth."

"So would I, but sometimes the truth isn't so clear." She smiled faintly, grateful that he was trying to understand. "As it so happens, I don't know if he had a gun or not. At the time, I was sure I'd seen one in his hand, even though a search afterward turned up nothing. But maybe I hated that man so bad I wanted to believe he was armed, just so I could erase his evil ass. Or maybe a few of my more bigoted fellow cops saw a perfect opportunity to get rid of a mouthy woman who refused to learn her place. Maybe the gun fell through a sewer grate or got lost behind a pile of trash, and someone walked away with it later. I know that's not the answer you want to hear.

"And ultimately, it doesn't matter to me if McConnell had a gun or not. He deserved to die, and I'm not sorry I killed him. But that's exactly why I don't deserve to wear a badge, and also why I never fought back during what happened afterwards."

Vincent fell silent for a moment. "I can't say I'm sorry you killed the bastard, either."

"Would *you* have shot him?"

"I don't know. I've never been in that kind of situation. I try to hold to a code of ethics, but I'm capable of killing under the right set of circumstances."

"Well, you're not alone in that. Not a lot of people were going to defend a man who'd raped and killed little girls and old women. There wasn't much genuine outrage after the shooting. It was Texas, the guy was headed for death row anyway; I just speeded up the process. I know there are dirty cops who do a lot worse.

I could've fought to keep my badge, but *I* knew I didn't deserve to wear it anymore."

"Ever think maybe you were too hard on yourself?"

Claudia shrugged. "You have your line in the sand, I have mine. I became a cop because I grew up in a rough neighborhood and I saw what happened to people who weren't strong enough or mean enough to take care of themselves. I wanted to look out for those people, and I figured it would be easier to do that with a badge and a gun."

"It *is* easier."

"Well, yeah, but see . . . I didn't get into it for duty or honor, for ethics or the Great American Dream. I was just mad, and not gonna sit back and do nothing about it." Claudia looked down. "When I was twelve, some neighborhood kid's cat got stuck in a drain and this older lady cop showed up to help. You could tell life hadn't been so good to her; she was just there for the paycheck. A few kids were being loud and disrespectful to her, but she didn't speak much Spanish and ignored them. It took her almost an hour to pry that stupid cat out of the sewer drain, and when she was walking back to her squad, one of those smart-ass kids threw a rock at her."

"So what happened?" Vincent prodded. "I assume she didn't shoot the brat."

"No, she didn't get mad, but *I* did. I yelled out this furious thank-you at her, in English. I remember how she looked at me, never smiling, and said 'you're welcome' in Spanish, and I knew it was her way of respecting me." Embarrassment rose, warming her face, because he was staring at her with a blank, unreadable expression. Like he thought she was crazy or something.

"Anyway, it made a big impression, because I realized even stupid little things like that could make a difference. From that day on, I made it my business to look out for the ones no one else looked after. I was the one the other kids went to when they had trouble with bullies. I was tall for my age, and I had a big, mean mouth."

She expected him to say something, but the silence lengthened, and he was still staring. She cleared her throat. "I guess I still have a big, mean mouth and I talk too much."

Vincent startled her when he leaned over and gave her a quick, light kiss on her temple. "I joined the FBI because I wanted the government bennies—and because I happen to have the above-average deductive reasoning skills they were looking for."

Claudia smiled. "And because you want to help and make a difference. You don't fool me."

"There is that," he admitted, smiling back.

Again, the awkward little silence—and, again, it was easier to fall back on light and casual. "So now you know all my deep, dark secrets," she said.

"I think I've barely scratched the surface." His gaze

roamed her body, lingering on her breasts, the juncture of her thighs. Then, with a sigh, he stood. "I had planned on joining you in the shower, but we both probably need some time apart to get all this straight in our heads."

Her heart sank. She'd gone too far, revealed too much. She'd heard the old we-need-some-time-apart excuse before. Stupid, stupid, to think he'd stick around if—

"Sex is always the easy part. It's the stuff that comes afterwards that can drive me crazy. I never know the right words to say, how to act," Vincent said as he dressed, his tone tinged with frustration. "But don't worry; we'll figure out a way to make it work. Like I said—above-average skills in problem solving."

Startled, Claudia stared at him. He *wasn't* skipping out on her? And what, exactly, did he mean by "all this"? Dammit; it was way too early in the morning for drama. "I'm not getting my hopes up."

It was admitting more than she liked, but the words were out before she thought better of it.

"Maybe it's about time you did." Vincent buttoned his shirt as he looked over at her.

For once, she let him get in the last word. After he'd left and she'd showered, she came back into the room, which didn't feel as lonely as before.

Was finding happiness as easy as this? A night of great sex with a man who was genuinely . . . nice?

The odds were stacked like hell against them. There was no way they could make a relationship work beyond a few quickies here and there.

Or *was* there a way? Her fighting instincts roused automatically at the tantalizing scent of a challenge.

It wasn't as if she'd be the first Avalon operative who had worked around a relationship obstacle. Case in point: Will Tiernay and Mia, his sweet little thing from Boston. If Tiernay could pull it off, why couldn't she? He was no better or worse than she was, though he did have a better-than-average talent for bending rules.

Huh . . . maybe it was time she tried a little more bending and a little less breaking.

Chapter Thirteen

"You have the most beautiful breasts. I could lie here all night and just look at them."

"If that's all you did, we wouldn't have nearly as much fun as we just did." Mia Dolan, still catching her breath, peered at her fiancé, Will, as he sprawled, chest still heaving, with his face buried in her cleavage. His dark hair tickled.

"True." His voice was muffled. "Doesn't change the fact that I like looking at 'em as much as I like playing with 'em."

"How very male of you."

Mia shifted so she could better appreciate how his long, muscular body stood out in contrast to her paler form. The bed was thoroughly wrecked, their clothing scattered on the floor. He'd arrived in London only a few hours ago; they hadn't wasted any time getting from Kings Cross to the hotel.

"For the record, you have a very fine bum and I very much enjoy looking at it, too."

He laughed, raising himself on his elbows to meet her gaze. "Listen to you. Back in London for a few days, and you've already reverted to native-speak."

"So I have." Lazily, she ran her heels along his legs to that splendid bum, goosing him with a heel and laughing when he yelped. "Are you up for another round, or shall we take a break? I *am* a little hungry."

"You're always hungry after sex, and I, not being twenty anymore, need to recuperate."

Regretfully, Mia noted twinges and aches that reminded her she wasn't a pliable twenty-something anymore, either. The first two times had been rather . . . enthusiastic.

Will rolled off her, stretched—much to her delight—then folded his hands behind his head. "I'm hungry, too. All I've had time to eat today was a scone and some lukewarm tea. You must've hit a pub or two with your old coworkers from the museum, right?"

"Oh, there was good food and good ale and good cheer aplenty," Mia said. "It was nice, but a little awkward, too."

"Ah. The subject of Vanessa must've come up."

Vanessa Sharpton had been her coworker and friend over the past five years. Now she was dead because Mia had foolishly chosen the wrong man to love.

"How'd you know?"

"Unavoidable, since they were her friends, too. Besides, I can always tell when you're thinking about her. You look like you're going to cry."

"Oh."

"You okay?" Will nudged her, gently. "I shouldn't have brought up her name. Sorry."

Mia gave him a quick, reassuring smile. "No, don't be sorry. It's okay. It was harder to deal with today, that's all, because I couldn't help but remember all the great times we had when we were living in London." She paused. "Then I couldn't stop remembering. I can still *feel* the heat from the explosion, you know? And as much as I hated what she'd done, to die like that is so horrible, and I—"

"You did nothing wrong. There's nothing to feel guilty about."

"I know." She inched closer against him. "I'm just hoping she didn't suffer, that's all."

Silence fell between them, Will's hold tightening in a comforting reminder that the ordeal was over. She focused on how companionable and cozy it felt to lie together in a dark room while London went its merry, noisy way outside and the sunlight began to fade. After a while, the shifting shadows lulled her into a calmer, more peaceful frame of mind.

Too bad this lovely contentment couldn't last. As usual, they had only a day or two before he flew off to Rome to do . . . whatever. His frequent absences were difficult, but they left her even more grateful for the moments when they were together again, no matter how brief.

"When you called, you said we'd only have a couple days in London instead of a week. Is everything okay?"

He nodded. "Yeah. It's just work being work."

She hesitated. "Is it something you can talk about?"

"I don't know. I want to, Mia, but—"

"It's dangerous," she finished, with a little sigh.

"Danger's always involved, but this time it's mostly . . . delicate." He ran a hand through his hair, leaving it spiky and disheveled.

"The usual offer stands. If you want to bounce thoughts off me, I'm here to listen and help where I can." Self-consciously, catching sight of herself in the mirror across the room, she smoothed back her own dark hair, feeling snarls among the curls. Messy might look sexy as hell on him, but it only looked scary on her. Eeek!

He watched, smiling at her efforts, then lifted a strand of her hair and coiled it around his index finger.

"Talking things out with you always helps." The satiated growl of his voice nearly reduced her to liquid all over again, and when he held out an arm, she scooted tight against him, reveling in the warmth of his nearness and comforting strength.

After a moment, he added, "What I miss most about not being a cop anymore is how I can't toss out ideas at others and see what bounces back. The lone wolf routine has its moments, but cooperative problem solving isn't one of them."

He absently caressed her hip. With a low sigh, he said, "The trouble is that I trusted Ben Sheridan to tell me the truth. I believed he'd been honest with me—until I was forced to start factoring in all the lies of omission."

"You're not really surprised by this, are you? I mean, he is what he is, right?"

"Yeah, but it still pisses me off."

Another little silence followed, then Mia pressed, carefully. "You also told me, when you called, that you'd taken an unplanned detour on the way back from Edinburgh. You went to West St. Aubry, didn't you? Where the Whitlea family used to live."

"The widow still lives in the old manor house," he answered after a moment.

"Is she all alone now?" Mia imagined a frail little old lady shuffling about an old, dank manor in her slippers and housecoat, with no company but cats and the memories of her dead husband and son.

"Isabel, the daughter, was only seven when her father and brother disappeared, and she's all grown up now, married and moved away. Ben's older sister, Ophelia, the one married to one of the Whitlea cousins, lives close by. They look after Mrs. Whitlea."

"That's nice of them." Clearly something was troubling Will, and Mia was torn between wanting to respect his need for keeping secrets and needing to be a full part of his life, the good as well as the bad. "Did you visit Mrs. Whitlea?"

"No, not yet. I'm going to have to do that very soon, though."

"Hmmm."

Will rolled his head, smiling. "You're fishing."

"I am, but only if you take the bait."

At that, he laughed. "I've been working on the murder of Maria Balestrini for months now, and I've still got nothing. Since she was killed back in the forties, in the middle of a world war, I expected things to be slow-going. I still can't see how she's connected to the Whitleas, but I figured that, to understand why Ben felt otherwise, I'd have to dig a little deeper into the Whitlea family itself. To say that I started turning up a few surprising details is to make a huge-ass understatement."

"This would be where all those lies of omission come in?"

"Yeah, and bald-faced, outright lies, too. Like how the second baronet didn't die in a drunken car crash in France. He disappeared in Nazi-occupied Poland in 1939. What he was doing there, I don't know, but two baronets from the same family disappearing into thin air, in the space of some sixty years, isn't a coincidence."

"I don't know, Will. It was right at the start of World War Two, and extreme events during times of war aren't unusual."

"Except I have information the guy wasn't some dumb bastard who wandered into a country full of Nazis, got himself shot, and was dumped in an anonymous hole in the ground. I'm talking murder, family secrets, and government officials covering up inconvenient truths—and some of this shit went down not all that long ago. Ben Sheridan is in it deep, and he was in it deep when he was only seventeen fuckin' years old."

"Uh-oh."

"Yeah, exactly . . . and Ben should've told me all of this, but he didn't. I have a pretty good idea why he's kept quiet, and it's also why I can't say much more to you about it now, because there are people who'd kill for this information. You've met some of these people. One of them threatened to blow you up in a factory unless I gave him what he wanted."

Mia met his gaze, widening her eyes as the significance of his words grew clearer. "Oh. My. God," she whispered.

Will shifted his focus to the ceiling. "And the frustrating part is that none of what I've discovered is going to help me find the sonofabitch who killed a pretty girl over sixty years ago and dumped her in a ditch. If I'm right, what I've discovered is who runs Avalon. You know Sheridan isn't going to be happy about that, yet he had to anticipate I might figure out the truth. So what does he *really* want from me?"

Mia blinked in startled confusion, uneasy. Ben Sheridan had always been polite to her, but something about the man had unsettled her from the moment she met him. "I don't know, Will. I really don't."

"I bet that nice old lady at Whitlea Manor knows," he muttered, his tone tight with anger. "And I'm going to get the truth from her this week. I'm done with running around in circles, and I'm tired of being played."

Chapter Fourteen

Friday morning, Philadelphia

Vincent was late—thirty minutes, to be exact.

Sitting in her rental, parked across the street from his house, Claudia scowled at his front door, as if that were enough to instantly conjure him from wherever he was at the moment. She didn't relish the idea of waiting much longer; the thick, humid air was already making her skin sticky and her hair frizz.

The heat wasn't stopping the neighborhood joggers, though. A blond housewife honey was bouncing along the sidewalk, breasts straining against a damp white tee, and her running shorts—which barely covered her butt cheeks—had writing across the back. Claudia squinted, trying to make out the words, until she realized she was staring at another woman's ass.

She opened the car slightly to catch any breeze and told herself to relax. Vincent was probably caught in traffic; she should just tip the seat back and grab a quick nap. Having sex into the wee hours of the morning was great, but now the lack of sleep was catching up with her. A sweet languor still weighed down her tired muscles, and she smiled.

Vincent had been very, *very* good to her. Too bad that while he seemed willing to make a go of a relationship, she wasn't so sure it would be worth the effort. Ben was pulling her out of Philly, and while she was certain she'd cross paths with Vincent again, she couldn't see a way around all the obstacles between them.

Last night, she'd been willing to hope. This morning, it seemed smarter to make a clean break. It would be easier on him, and easier on her as well. If she were a cop or an FBI agent, it might be different, but working for Avalon wasn't exactly ideal for hooking up with a guy who wasn't already a coworker, understood the lifestyle, and accepted what came with it.

The realization didn't improve her mood any, and she absently watched cars zip along the street. Men and women off to work for the day, taking the kids to school or day care. The jogger with the distracting shorts ran by again, and when she stopped in front of Vincent's house to retie her shoelaces, Claudia could finally read the words on her back end: A WORK OF ART.

Hello, ego.

The woman resumed her jog and Claudia briefly tracked her, amused in spite of herself, before checking her watch again.

How long should she wait? She was hungry but hadn't grabbed anything from the hotel's continental breakfast tables before heading out, expecting to eat at Vincent's. If he didn't show up in the next twenty minutes, she'd leave him a note and go find a McDonald's to quiet the grumbles in her stomach. If she waited too long to eat and slug back her morning hit of caffeine, she'd get the shakes.

As she waited, she occupied herself by mulling over everything Vincent had told her last night about the security data.

It was a lot more than they'd had before, when combined with what she'd turned up. They were dealing with more than one thief, the thieves were taking the easiest opportunities, were at least a little smarter than average, and were careful planners. Knowing this boosted her mood, since chasing down smart targets was a lot more challenging and exciting.

When her belly let out a long rumble, she tried calling Vincent's office but got his voice mail. She sighed and rummaged in her purse for a piece of paper and a pen to leave him a note. Halfway through the note, she noticed the jogger with the work-of-art ass pass by Vincent's house once more. She'd stopped again by his driveway, this time to gulp down some water.

Instincts snapping to attention, Claudia stared closely at the woman, whose face struck her as vaguely familiar. This didn't feel right at all—and what a bad time to have gone conscientious and left her gun in the hotel room. She slipped out of the car and started across the street, trying to keep as quiet as possible, but something must've caught the woman's attention, because she suddenly spun around, eyes widening.

In a split second, Claudia realized where she'd seen her: in the hotel bar last night with the drunk Amazon who'd nearly knocked her over.

Except last night this woman had been a brunette, not a blonde.

"Hey!" Claudia quickened her pace. "Who the hell are you and— Oh, *fuck!*"

The woman turned and bolted, rabbit-fast. Claudia followed, pushing herself to match the speed. The woman weaved through parked cars, hedges, and trees, forcing Claudia to slow down. Her breathing was labored already, and a mix of embarrassment and anger shot through her, giving her an extra boost of speed. She began to close in. Just as she realized the woman was heading toward a small playground, she heard the squeal of tires as a car braked hard. Distantly, she heard someone call her name.

Vincent.

It had to be, and the sudden cacophony of car horns, followed by a gunning engine, told her she'd guessed right.

Not that he'd be much help, with Miss Arty Ass zipping toward a playground.

A car began backing out of a driveway, and the woman jumped, landing on the trunk and launching herself to the sidewalk on the other side. The driver braked, car rocking, staring openmouthed as Claudia darted fast behind him, opting against the airborne route.

The playground was in plain view now, and the woman turned up the speed even more. Her lungs and muscles burning, Claudia matched it, her longer legs eating up the distance between them. Behind her, she heard running footsteps but didn't break her momentum to look back.

A young mother pushing a stroller emerged from behind a small hedge, right into the runner's path. Claudia shouted, "Look out!" The startled mother turned on instinct, hunching protectively over the baby, and took the full force of the glancing collision.

The mother fell, managing to keep the stroller from toppling. The runner stumbled but kept her footing, and barely broke her stride. Claudia ran past the frightened mother, who was now clutching her bawling infant. A quick look assured her neither was hurt. Vincent wasn't far behind her; she trusted him to take care of the situation if necessary.

Even more angry now, Claudia pushed herself all-out. She didn't bother wasting breath to yell "Stop"; once she got close enough, she'd tackle the bitch.

Swing sets and playground equipment passed in a

blur. A street corner lay just ahead, busy with traffic. Arty Ass would have to slow down, and then Claudia would *have* her.

Claudia heard Vincent's shouted waning at the same moment she glimpsed a flash of white out of the corner of her eye. A body slammed into her, knocking her off-balance and sending her skidding down the sidewalk.

Rough concrete scoured away her flesh, but she had the presence of mind to roll, tucking in her head, until she finally came to a stop. Despite the pain, despite the world spinning wildly around her, she pulled herself into an unsteady crouch and looked up. It took a moment for her eyes to focus, but she found them: two women, one tall and one short, racing away, distance rapidly shrinking them smaller and smaller . . .

The dizziness took her under, sudden and swift, and she fell back on the grass, gasping. No, no, she would *not* faint; it would be too damn embarrassing!

Over the sound of her harsh breathing came the howling of an angry baby and the thud of running footsteps, much closer. Vincent shouted, "Claudia! Jesus, are you all right?"

"Second time that bitch has body-slammed me," she mumbled as he reached her.

"Are you all right, Claudia?"

"Yeah," she said, sitting up with his help. "Except I left half my skin on the sidewalk. Ow, *ow!*"

"You're bleeding."

"No shit," she snapped.

He made a strange sound—a laugh?—and then demanded, "Is anything broken?"

"I don't know." The screaming baby caught her attention again, and she asked, "Is the kid okay? And the mother?"

"Yeah, I stopped to make sure of that."

"I knew you would." She closed her eyes with a wince. Damn, she *hurt*.

As his fingers firmly searched out any broken bones, she closed her eyes and gritted her teeth, determined not to groan or yell. She was always a wuss when it came to pain. Humiliating, but true.

Sound fuzzed in and out, and she forced herself to stay upright, to focus. She could hear Vincent on his cell phone, talking to a police dispatcher.

Maybe she'd get lucky and a patrol would find those two women and haul them to lockup. At the sound of sirens, her eyes snapped open. "I don't need an ambulance. Just help me back to your place so we can talk."

"Too late. They're already on their way. Dammit, sit still! I can't feel anything broken, but let them do their job and check you over."

The sirens were much closer, and she scowled. "I'm not going to the hospital."

"Fine, but let them check you out."

He was splitting his focus between her and the mother and baby. The stroller lay on its side in the grass, likely knocked over when the mother yanked out her baby. The woman paced in a tense, tight circle as she jiggled the baby and patted its pink, diaper-puffy bottom. A crowd had gathered, and several women were comforting the distraught mother.

"Claudia." His voice sounded ever more terse than before. "Claudia, look at me."

She obeyed, though it took an effort to focus. His expression was a mix of anger and worry. He looked so safe and solid, and the concern in his dark eyes made her insides twist in a little pang. All she wanted was to crawl into his arms, close her eyes, and make the world go away for a few minutes.

Instead, she went for flip: "What's with the hollering and the worried looks? It takes more than skidding across concrete to hurt me."

"You *are* hurt, you dumb-ass," he snapped. "And what the hell was all that about? What's going on?"

"We need to discuss this in private," she said as three EMTs hurried toward her. At Vincent's gesture, one veered off toward the mother. "Those women were at the hotel bar last night. The tall one bumped into me and nearly knocked me down. I'm thinking it wasn't by accident."

Surprise flashed in his eyes, but the EMTs had arrived and the time for questions passed. A patrol car pulled up shortly after that, and Claudia spent what seemed like hours answering questions when she wasn't swearing and hissing in pain as the EMTs disinfected and dressed her raw, oozing scrapes. Her knees and elbows had taken the brunt of her fall and hurt like hell. She finally got to her feet, slowly, as one of the EMTs supported her.

Vincent abruptly walked away from the cop and joined her, slipping a strong, solid arm around her. Gratefully, Claudia leaned against him. She provided the cop with descriptions of the two women but didn't tell him that she'd encountered them the night before.

Finally, the crowds dispersed. As the ambulance and patrol car pulled away, Vincent turned to her. "Can you walk?"

"Yeah. Just go slow. Nothing's broken, but my ankle's not right. Must've twisted it a little."

"Okay. I'm parked over there."

He waved toward a distant clump of trees, but Claudia only nodded, not bothering to look. Five feet or five thousand, it was going to be a painful walk, limping along clumsily with Vincent's arm around her.

After a minute he stopped, bringing her to a halt. "This isn't working. Get on my back."

"What?"

He hunkered down in front of her and motioned at his back. "Get on. I'll piggyback you to the car."

"Vincent, that's sweet and all, but I'm not exactly a featherweight and—"

"Shut up and climb on."

Anger flared but quickly turned to amusement. "Way to go with the smooth talking, DeLuca."

He simply waited.

She rolled her eyes. She could continue to argue, but this was something he clearly needed to do. And, in all honesty, it would feel nice to lean on someone for a change. She didn't allow herself that luxury very often. Swallowing her bruised pride, she wrapped her legs around his waist and leaned against his back.

"I haven't done this since I was like . . . six or something," she said as he slid his arms firmly under her knees and hoisted her up. His muscles bunched and hardened beneath her as he stood.

"Hang on." Vincent set off down the sidewalk at a brisk pace. The awkward silence that followed was broken by his quiet laugh. "I'd been thinking all morning about getting between your legs again, but this isn't exactly what I had in mind."

Claudia blinked, surprised by his bluntness, then realized he was trying to distract her, to cheer her up.

"Aw, that's so sweet."

His shoulders shook as he laughed again. "You sure have a unique view of what's sweet, Claudia. You're one of a kind."

"Thank you for noticing. It's about damn time." She leaned fully against him, wrapping her arms around his neck and resting her head against his. "I'm getting blood all over your suit."

"I've got others."

She smiled into his hair and tightened her hold a little more. "I figured as much. A hundred of 'em, all exactly the same."

"Listen to you, sassing off at a man who can drop you on your ass." He grinned. "Which means you're okay."

Again, that funny little flutter deep inside. "I told you so."

"When you said you'd seen those two before, I was thinking maybe you'd hit your head."

"Nope . . . and the one I was chasing? Last night, she was a brunette."

As her meaning sank in, his body tensed. He glanced back, holding her gaze. "Is that so?"

"Uh-huh. The big one that hit me, she's tall enough to pass for a man. I didn't get a good look at her face, though. Didn't last night, either." She paused. "You got the security stuff with you?"

"Yup."

"Good." She sighed. "And remind me to tell you why I think those women know who I am to begin with."

He shot her another quick look. "Count on it."

Chapter Fifteen

"Ow!" Claudia yelped. "Ow, ow, ow . . . goddammit, DeLuca, that hurts!"

"I didn't think you'd be such a freakin' big baby about this."

She bounced a little in agony, sitting on the toilet seat in his bathroom. He'd insisted on changing the bandages because she'd bled through them, and she'd been fighting it from the start. "It *stings!*"

"Of course it does," he retorted. "Now stop squirming. This is hard enough as it is, and I don't like hurting you. If you'd gone to the hospital, as I'd suggested—"

"No." She glared. "Make fun of me all you want, but I have a ginormous needle phobia."

He tried not to grin, because he was pretty certain she'd deck him if he told her he found her panic cute, in a weird sort of way. She was so tough; who'd have thought she'd freak out over scraped knees or the sight of a needle?

"I wouldn't make fun of you." He began bandaging her knees. He'd finished with her elbows and the raw spot on her chin, but the knees looked the worst. "I suggest you make friends with a bottle of Tylenol or Advil starting now, because tomorrow you'll really be hurting."

"I know. God, I can't wait to get my hands on that woman who hit me. I owe her some serious payback." Then, trying to check herself in the mirror, she asked, "Do I look really bad?"

"Good to see your ego survived undamaged," Vincent said, caught between exasperation and amusement. "You look fine for someone who went skidding across concrete. It could be a lot worse."

She winced as she touched her chin. "This had better not leave a scar or I'm gonna kill her."

"So how about explaining what you think is going on here?"

"The woman I was chasing was watching your place. At first I didn't pick up on it—I mean, it's not like I was expecting you to have your own pair of stalkers."

"Me, either," he said grimly.

"So the first time she jogged by, I didn't really notice. I probably wouldn't have noticed at all if she hadn't had A WORK OF ART written across her ass. Even *my* ego's not that big." She shared a grin with him. "And when she stopped outside your place, tying her shoe, I didn't think anything of it. But when she stopped the second time, there was no way it could be a coincidence."

"And you're sure you saw this same woman at the hotel bar last night?" Vincent asked as he carefully tied off the ends of the gauze bandages.

"Positive. I got a good look at her face when she turned around after her pal almost knocked me over. She recognized me, too; that's why she took off."

Vincent stood. "So you think they're watching *me*?"

"Gotta be. They might've followed you last night to the bar." Claudia frowned. "Do you remember when I told you how I had set up a meeting with Digger Brody and he didn't show?"

It took him a few seconds to place the name. "Yup."

"Well, it crossed my mind at the time that he stood me up on purpose so someone could get a good look at me."

"And lo and behold, these two literally run into you shortly after that. They might have been at the hotel for you, not me."

"Maybe."

"I don't like this."

"Can't say I like it much, either. It's taking the usual theft for fun and profit in a direction that's not so usual. Or fun." Her frown deepened. "Vincent, was anybody from the Art Squad a guest speaker at that convention last night?"

"I don't think so. Why?"

"You told me the other night you've given talks in

public, right?" When he nodded, she added, "To industry people, I'm sure. Museums, universities, galleries, auction houses. Where did you give those talks?"

He knew instantly where she was going with this. "Jesus," he said softly. "I gave talks in every city where there was a theft."

"So it looks like the connection in these cases, Vincent, is *you*. Even the detour interest in me is because of you."

He sat down against the tub, running through the events of the last four months, replaying in his mind where he'd given those talks. There was no doubt about it: In every city he'd lectured, a theft had followed within a few weeks.

"You're telling me that all the time I've been giving talks on how to protect art collections, I might also have been giving pointers to thieves on how to circumvent those protections?"

She shrugged. "Don't know their motivation yet, but don't be too hard on yourself. I doubt you've said anything that they couldn't already read on a half dozen art and museum sites on the Net. The security issues aren't exactly a big secret, and museums and galleries are open to the public and therefore harder to protect. I really don't think stealing is the point; it's *you* they're interested in."

The thought made his skin crawl. "Why?"

"Again, I don't know. My best guess is that they're

trying to catch your attention. I don't suppose you've noticed any regular attendees at those lectures of yours?"

Vincent sifted through his memories. "I doubt they would have come to any of them. These talks are directed to very specific audiences. I would've noticed if the same faces kept showing up."

"But it's not likely a coincidence, Vincent. Were those talks publicized?"

"Sure, for industry insiders. Anyone could find the talk schedules posted on museum security news sites. The seminars weren't intended to be secret."

"So they pull off a showy little job in every place you give your spiel, as a fuck-you of sorts, I guess, but they don't get your attention. Then they start stalking you."

"Well, if they wanted my attention, they got it now."

As he spoke, something about the phrasing rang familiar. Something he should remember, something important.

"I think we need to talk to Digger Brody again," she said.

"Yeah," Vincent agreed absently, trying to pin down the memory. Something about attention, getting it, keeping it . . .

Then it came to him: the blonde at the bar, the one who'd known his name. She'd asked for his name from the bar owner's kid, but if what Claudia proposed was true, asking might have been for show, because she'd known it all along.

Candy, she'd called herself. The blonde in the flowery dress who'd said, *I may have to do something dramatic for that to happen.*

She'd been complaining about a man who didn't notice her because he was wrapped up in another woman.

"Let's go look at that security data," he said abruptly.

Claudia flashed him a startled glance. "Fine. Don't tell me I'm brilliant."

"You're brilliant," he said automatically.

She made a face at him. "Okay. The sooner we get through the recordings, the closer I am to getting my hands on those two. Help me up? Aaaah, ouchies, *ouchies!*"

Vincent laughed; he couldn't help it. He kept expecting her to act more like a Marine and less like a kid who'd fallen off her bike.

He glanced at her clothes, then at his own, bloodied and grass-stained. They could also both use a shower, but clean clothing was a higher priority.

After settling her on the couch, Vincent motioned toward the stairs leading to the second story and his bedroom. "I'll get something for you to wear and throw these clothes in the laundry. Then I'll make a pizza and we can start going over those recordings."

"Pizza?" She stared at him. "It's morning."

"True, but I don't usually eat breakfast at home, and the only thing I have in the house is pizza."

She shrugged. "Okay. I'll take whatever I can get."

Soon, dressed in clean clothes, sniffing appreciatively at the smell of baking pizza, he and Claudia sat side by side and watched fuzzy security data. He started with the tape from Champion and Stone, which he knew practically by heart.

"They're deliberately hiding their faces as they pass the camera . . . see how he—or she—pretends to cough here?" Claudia asked, pointing. "And in this one, her hair is obscuring her face. They knew exactly where the cameras were. Also, that woman who came back to look for her watch? Maybe she should've been looking for a purse instead—because she had one when she showed up but I didn't see it with her when she left."

"What?" Vincent stared at her, realizing he'd missed something important. Swearing under his breath, he quickly checked the frames and saw that he had indeed missed that little detail. Caught up in Gray Suit and the dark-haired woman, he'd missed the obvious. "There's the other half of the tag team, then."

"Looks that way."

"Can't believe I missed it.

Claudia shrugged. "Nobody's perfect. We've got the info now, and I think we're beginning to see what's going on here. Do you have anything earlier from Champion and Stone? I wanna see if these two show up again."

Vincent shook his head. "Nope. You know how it is; despite repeated warnings to step up security, funds are tight and security gets the short end. They don't want anyone walking out with a da Vinci, but they also don't want visitors having to go through security that would put federal penitentiaries to shame."

Claudia grunted. "Too bad, because people *are* walking off with da Vincis and van Goghs . . . hell, Munch's *The Scream* has been stolen twice over the past fifteen years."

"We always get it back." Vincent scratched his chin. "I prefer cases involving high-profile art. It's impossible to sell those pieces in any legitimate market, so they usually turn up again right away. It's thieves like these two that give me ulcers. The little stuff . . . man, it's hard to get it back once it's gone. But you probably know all about that. It's one reason why none of us have managed to snag the infamous Rainert von Lahr."

"Tell me about it," Claudia said, with feeling. "Not that he hasn't been involved in some high-profile thefts, but like our girls here, he usually goes for the more obscure pieces. Trading around the small stuff is more profitable for him, not to mention smarter than trying to sell a Renoir or a Picasso."

"And he's also smart enough to handle thefts through intermediaries." Vincent knew of von Lahr but had never been involved in any of the investigations where he'd been identified as a suspect. The FBI's last direct lead on von Lahr in the United States had followed a botched attempt to smuggle a stolen dinosaur fossil out of the country, and Vincent hadn't even been working the Art Squad when that happened.

"One of these days, we'll get him. We may be chasing him around with walkers and bifocals, but we'll get him." Claudia sat back, sifting through papers and screen-shot printouts for his notes. "Hmmm, let's look at the security from the Baltimore theft. I want to focus on the most recent ones because I think that's where we're seeing the escalating interest in you."

Smiling at the thought of ancient FBI and Avalon agents chasing von Lahr with walkers, Vincent pulled out the data from the Baltimore gallery theft and loaded it.

Not even two minutes in, Claudia suddenly straightened. "There. The blonde in the business suit." Vincent quickly hit the Pause button, and then advanced slowly through each subsequent frame. "She drops her earring, and the clerk, being a nice person, helps her look for it—"

"—while this woman walks right past without being noticed," Vincent finished. As he studied the screen more closely, a chill washed over him. "Is this your Amazon?"

Claudia leaned forward, peering at the blurred image. "Hard to say. Height looks about right, but she's bulked up her body to look fat . . . and again with the trick of obscuring the face."

"What about the blonde? You recognize her?" he asked, trying to keep his voice neutral.

She turned, narrowing her eyes, then glanced at the

screen before turning back to him again. "Could be the woman I was chasing. What's wrong?"

"I recognize her. I'm fairly sure it's the same woman who sat down beside me at a bar a few nights ago."

"Oh, boy," Claudia said after a moment. "That's it, then. I was hoping I might be wrong, cuz it *is* a pretty wacky theory, but if she walked right up to you like that, there's no doubt. Tell me about her, Vincent."

He filled her in and they both sat back, thinking and eating their pizza. Vincent became aware of a growing sense of companionable comfort, the kind that came from a team that clicked. If it hadn't been for Claudia, he never would've known he was being followed by two women who were likely the thieves he'd been chasing for months.

Or he wouldn't have known until it was too late. He doubted their intentions toward him were friendly; Claudia might have just saved his ass.

"It's like they're playing a game with you."

"A one-sided game, if the other party has no idea what's going on."

"You probably would've figured it out before too long, and if you didn't, they would've made it more obvious. Why else take the risk of approaching you in a bar? Or starting in on me?"

"It seems pretty damn risky to steal just to get the attention of the man who'll throw you in prison for the crime. What do they hope to accomplish?"

Claudia looked worried. "We need to lean on Brody. He definitely knows more than he's letting on."

"I'll take care of that right now." Three calls later, Vincent said, "All set. City cops are on the lookout for Brody and will bring him in for questioning as soon as they find him."

"It does help to have the cred of an FBI agent," Claudia said, a twinge of envy in her tone.

Vincent gave a jaw-cracking yawn, then sighed. "This is crazy. Wouldn't it be a hell of a lot easier to ambush me and tie me up? It's not like I had any idea I was being followed."

"Pretty ballsy of them, stalking an FBI agent. These girls got moxie, for sure."

"Let's watch the rest of the recordings. I think we're about to find a pattern and ID some faces."

The morning wore on as they watched feed after feed, shoulder to shoulder and head to head, saying little.

Several of the recordings provided glimpses of what had now become familiar enough behavior to convince him they were on the right track. "There she is again," he said quietly as they watched the feed from the Washington, DC, theft. "The Amazon makes a convincing man."

"She sure does," Claudia said. "The games bad people play. Ain't it fun?"

Chapter Sixteen

"How are you doing over there?"

Claudia looked up from the pile of case notes she'd been reading. They were just like Vincent, detailed and straightforward. "Your notes won't be making any bestseller lists, but we're getting somewhere, so I don't mind if they're a little dull."

"Cute, but I was asking how *you're* feeling." He stood and stretched, taking a break from working on a time line to connect the thefts to his various talks. "How's your knees and elbows?"

"Not bad. It'll be the missionary position for me for a few days, though."

"That's *not* what I meant."

She grinned. It was so easy to rile that touchy male defensiveness, which made it hard to resist teasing him. "Just saying. You know you're thinking about it."

"Thinking and doing aren't the same. I'm not about to take advantage of a woman in pain."

"Why not? Most men seem to feel sex will cure everything."

"I don't know about cure, but it does tend to make everything better," Vincent admitted, grinning.

Sometimes, for such a sharp man, he could be incredibly dense. "So you're not gonna offer to kiss my boo-boos and make everything all better with *your* sex fu?"

Vincent laughed, but the sudden gleam in his dark eyes told her he was finally getting the picture. "Sex fu is your territory. I'm just the guy who can't resist a lady in distress. Give me your hand and I'll help you up."

The truth was, she hurt something awful. Deep scrapes like hers exposed nerve endings, and the pain had hunkered down into a constant ache that pounded and throbbed. Despite her best efforts, it was hard to concentrate on little details, which pretty much described everything they'd been working on.

"Are we taking a break?" she asked, hoping she didn't sound too eager.

"Seems like a good idea. We've got plenty to work on already." He motioned at a neater pile of text and color photo prints. "I want to get that to the office. I'll run the pictures and see if we can come up with an ID. I'm not expecting much, but we might get lucky.

I also need to send the descriptions to the police so they can keep an eye out for our two suspects. I don't think we'll see either of them in my neighborhood again, now that they know we're aware of them, but it won't hurt to have a squad drive by now and then. I'm not sure there's much else we can do here."

Claudia knew he was right. "I have to get back to my hotel," she said with a sigh. "The office should've delivered my itinerary and assignment details by now. I really do have to fly out to Texas tomorrow."

He nodded in understanding. "I've got a trip coming up to Columbia, South Carolina, and I need to get to work on a few reports. This case may be personal now, and I need to get to the bottom of it because of that, but I also have a lot of other work piling up. I never seem to get ahead." He hesitated. "When you're done in Texas, will you be coming back here?"

"As soon as I can. I promise," Claudia said, no longer in the mood to be dodgy about her need to be with him. What was the point? Maintaining a relationship like this would be hard enough; why pointlessly complicate things? "I'm not sure how long I'll be gone, but I can give you a call and let you know when I'll be back. When are you heading out to Columbia?"

"Next Friday. I'll probably be down there all week, preparing for a trial."

"Ooh, fun."

"Oh, yeah. I just love trials." He hesitated again,

brows pulling together, then said, "Hey . . . I've been thinking that maybe you shouldn't go back to your hotel tonight."

"Why? I'm not the one being stalked by a couple of crazy, cross-dressing chicks."

"We don't know that for sure," he reminded her. "We *do* know they're aware of your connection to me, and where you're staying. I have no idea what they want from me, but it's not much of a stretch to assume they might see you as a threat to their plans." He motioned to her bandages. "I'd say it's pretty clear their intentions toward you aren't exactly friendly."

"So you're suggesting I switch to another hotel for tonight?"

"Or stay with me."

She laughed. "And that's supposed to be safer for me, how?"

"Do you really think they'd come back after today's chase? The element of surprise is gone; we know who they are, now."

"Maybe you and me should get a hotel room somewhere else instead. How does that sound?"

"Nice, but not practical." He took her hand, gently massing her fingers. "I want you to stay the night, Claudia. What do you say?"

Mmmm, the man had a magical touch, even in such small ways.

"Love to, but I still need to go back to my hotel.